THIS WOMAN WANTED

Rae Foley

A DELL BOOK

Published by
DELL PUBLISHING CO., INC.
750 Third Avenue
New York, New York 10017

Copyright © 1971 by Rae Foley

All rights reserved. No part of this book
may be reproduced in any form without permission
in writing from Dodd, Mead & Company.

Dell ® TM 681510, Dell Publishing Co., Inc.

Reprinted by arrangement with
Dodd, Mead & Company
New York, New York, 10016

Printed in the United States of America

First Dell printing—May 1972

THE IMPOSTER

Helen knew her husband, Will, had warned her not to try to see him. But she could stay alone no longer. It was no longer enough to glimpse him in the distance and watch him wave reassuringly before he swiftly disappeared.

Now, inside this abandoned shack on the edge of town, she saw him coming toward her in the dim light, wearing the loud sports coat she knew so well, and his familiar dark glasses.

Suddenly her mind screamed out a warning: **Dark glasses, in this dim light . . . ?** She snatched at the glasses and jerked them off . . . and before her was the hideous, hate-distorted face of a stranger . . . then a hard male fist exploding . . . and all was blackness. . . .

ONE

I saw him for the third time that Sunday morning while waiting for the manager to pick up the keys. In the past six months I must have inspected dozens of apartments, all of which sounded alike in the advertising columns: "One-bedroom apartment, furnished, air conditioning, heated pool." Actually, the places ran the gamut from rundown makeshifts to luxury living. What I wanted was to steer a middle course, not too bad, not too good, just average enough so as not to attract attention or arouse speculation. Not that it really mattered. I always took an apartment that did not require a lease because, sooner or later, someone recognized me and I moved on.

In all those months I had not heard his voice and I had seen him only twice until that morning. If it had not been for the letters, I would have distrusted the evidence of my eyes and believed, like everyone else, that he was dead. But always, within a day of my moving to a new address, a letter came, making it possible for me to go on a little longer.

And now, for the third time in six months, I saw him. He was across the wide boulevard and the sun was in my eyes, almost blinding me, but, though his flaming red hair was covered by a cap, there was no mistaking the oddly shaped frames of his dark glasses, the loudly checked sports jacket, and the achingly familiar gesture with which he sketched a salute as he turned away.

All the controls of all those months seemed to snap and I started toward him across the small wooden bridge that arched over running water to make up part of the Polynesian setting of the building when the manager came running back. She was about my own age, twenty-three, with a long oval face and the tight jeans and sloppy shirt that are almost a uniform in Southern California. She was also extremely pretty and she had a friendly, breezy manner. I liked her at once.

"I'm so sorry to keep you waiting," she said breathlessly, "but there was a tenant on the phone and she went on and on. I just had to listen. You know how it is, Miss—uh—"

"Brown," I said, and turned reluctantly from the elusive figure across the boulevard who was already moving away from me.

Bamboo slats were used as an imitation siding and there was an imitation Polynesian roof; water spilled noisily over stones and ran gurgling under the bridge and was stocked with goldfish.

"This looks attractive," I said.

"Well, actually, the main building is filled up; not a single vacancy. Mostly retired people on a long lease. But we do have some little cottages at the back where the swimming pool is. I think they are real cute. And we don't plan to ask tenants to sign a lease. We figured we might get some young people out there to pep things up, and they aren't always able to sign up for a long time, the way they move around, and they don't often have their own furniture."

I followed her through an archway to a patio in back. A heated pool was surrounded by beach chairs and metal tables and plastic lounges for sunbathing. There were palm trees and bushes laden with red and pink and white camellias, and there were half a dozen brightly painted cottages, set at odd angles as though they had been scattered around by sheer chance. The whole thing was a gay riot of color and I thought with a pang how Will would have loved it.

The little pink cottage which the manager showed me was pleasantly furnished and sunlit. Beyond the windows at the back I could see the line of mountains clearly etched against the sky, like two-dimensional cardboard mountains in a stage set. On a telephone wire outside the open windows a mockingbird mused over all the songs he had heard that morning.

"I'll take it."

"Oh, good!" The young manager's face lighted up as though she was genuinely pleased. "Are you planning to be here long, Miss Brown?"

"I never make plans." That God knows, was true.

"I hope you won't be nervous or lonely out here by yourself. My husband and I have just fixed up the cottages and you are the first to rent one of them. But any time you want someone to talk to, come up to the main building. There's always coffee going in my apartment and someone dropping in. And behind that bamboo hedge out at the back you'll find a real cute thatched hut with grills for steaks or hamburgers or barbecues. Rustic tables and benches and lanterns and everything. If you want to entertain, you can use it any time."

"That's very kind." I signed traveler's checks for a month's rent, hoping I'd be able to stay that long in the sunny little cottage. With the disposition of a domestic cat I wasn't emotionally cut out for this life of vagabondage and rootless drifting. My streak of adventure was so dim it wasn't discernable to the naked eye. It's people like me for whom women's magazines are written, with fascinating new recipes and ideas for home decoration. Women who want to stay put and plant a garden and know their neighbors and gossip over the back fence and have a place where their children can grow up and make friends of their own and have something to come back to, as a kind of anchor, after they have branched out on their own, so they need never feel entirely alone. Women whose husbands come home every evening.

Instead, I moved on from one furnished place to

another, always expecting someone to recognize me or to have a policeman's hand come down on my shoulder. And only three times in six months had I so much as caught a glimpse of my husband.

"You can move in today, if you like," the manager said. "I'll turn your refrigerator on. There's a good shopping center in the next block and you can buy things here on Sunday, you know."

"Yes, I know."

"Oh, I thought—well, traveler's checks and all—you might be a stranger." She looked at me, half smiling, half questioning, but completely friendly. "And yet I guess you aren't quite a stranger. You're sort of familiar, if you know what I mean. Like I've seen you before somewhere. And out here, of course, the first thing we think of when we recognize a face is the movies or television."

"I'm not an actress."

"Resemblances are funny, aren't they? Did anyone ever say you look kind of like Princess Grace?" She broke off, listening. "Excuse me, that's my little boy. I've got to run. Here are your keys. Any way I can help—about where to get things and all that—and my husband is real handy, too." She waved her hand and ran through the patio and under the archway to an open door marked MANAGER.

I was not far behind her when she entered her apartment and lifted a small boy with a robustly protesting voice and the bluest eyes I had ever seen out of a playpen and tossed him in the air, laughing. With the tears still wet on his cheeks, he laughed back. She seemed to take motherhood as lightly and gaily as she did her job of manager, and she called, " 'By now," as I went past.

I rolled down the windows of my anonymous little Volkswagen and turned back to check on the number of my new address. While keeping a wary eye on fast and heavy traffic, I tried to find a familiar figure across the boulevard, but he had gone; there was no one now.

Nor was there anyone in sight when I got back to the apartment where I had lived for the past three weeks. I had been half afraid to find my landlord lurking, as he had a way of doing, appearing whenever I ventured out of doors. A man with an invitation in his eyes and in his voice. That was one of the unpleasant problems I had learned to deal with during the first weeks of this nomad existence. Unattached young women drifting around in the general vicinity of Hollywood without a job or a known source of income are regarded as natural prey. It seemed odd that Will had not considered what my position was bound to be. Dearly as I loved him, there were times when I resented fiercely being pitchforked into situations where I had to fend off impertinent advances. I understood and accepted, up to a point, the fact that it was for my own safety, but there were times when I was tempted to walk into the nearest police station and give myself up, because it would be such a relief not to have to run any more.

I packed my two suitcases without waste motion, a routine at which I had become so adept that I could almost have done in the dark. After a final check of clothes closet and bureau drawers I went out to the Volkswagen and put my suitcases in the trunk.

This time I wasn't so lucky. The woman from the apartment above me had just parked her car in the next slot. She reached in to lift out a brown-paper bag of groceries and a carton of beer cans, and turned to give me a wide, friendly smile. She was, as she had informed me the first time I encountered her, a widow, but she was far from being solitary. Loud bursts of uninhibited laughter came from her apartment at all hours. Repeatedly she had tried to persuade me to join her parties. Her boy friend had a friend who would like to meet me. "You know how it is, honey; like they say, gentlemen prefer blondes." I think my continued refusals had hurt and puzzled her, but she bore me no rancor.

"Well, here you are just in time, Miss Brown! My

boy friend is bringing along this guy I've been telling you about. We're going to have some beer and toasted cheese sandwiches. Now you come right along. Les would cheer you up. It's anything for a laugh with Les."

There was, as far as I could detect, no lurking suspicion in her manner, no particular curiosity. The invitation was just what it claimed to be. I thanked her and explained that I was in the process of moving out.

"Now that's a shame!" she exclaimed warmly. "Just when we are getting acquainted so nice. Found a place you like better, dear?"

"No, I'm leaving town. My mother is ill and she asked me to come." Sometimes it amused me to learn how easily the lies came to me. A few months earlier I would have felt much too guilty to sound convincing.

"I'm sure sorry to hear it," she said with ready sympathy. "I hope you'll find everything all right. I told my boy friend I thought you'd been looking sort of down in the mouth lately and we ought to do something to cheer you up and he said— Well, anyhow, I certainly hope you'll find your mother on the mend. Was it something sudden, dear?"

It had been sudden. It always was. When the man with the white Pontiac had appeared the day before, I'd known I would have to move on again. True, he had made no attempt to bother me. He had been tinkering with his car when I returned from one of the movies where I spent most of my afternoons. He hadn't said much, just, "Nice day, isn't it, Mrs. Gates?"

I took my time locking the Volkswagen. My voice was steady, with just the right amount of coolness, when I replied, "Sorry. You've made a mistake."

"Have I?" He wasn't rude. In fact, his manner was as casual and relaxed as though my identity did not matter in the least. He was a little over average height, with a straight back and good shoulders and a brown skin as though he spent most of his time in the sun. He was about Will's age, thirty, but he seemed older in a way. A quiet man with an unstressed but unmistakable assurance as though he was on the best of terms with himself and his world.

I suppose psychiatrists have a word for it—they have for practically everything—and it is probably the wrong word. They never seem to think in terms of normal people with a sound, healthy psyche, the kind of people who don't have to follow trends or mouth other people's slogans to feel secure. This man even dared to have his hair trimmed and he was cleanly shaven. In California that makes any man look like Cary Grant without half trying.

There had been other people who had recognized me, particularly in those first weeks when my picture kept cropping up in the papers and on the television screen, so I had become accustomed to parrying questions. But this man frightened me, perhaps because he did not insist that he was right. He acted as though he could afford to play a waiting game and watch for me to make a mistake. One look at his hard eyes and the unyielding lines of his mouth and jaw was enough to tell me that he wasn't the man to abandon the chase. So I was relieved to slip into traffic that Sunday without being detected by him.

Not far from the apartment I was leaving there was a quiet restaurant with superlative food, which is as rare in Southern California as it is commonplace in San Francisco. It was one of those places kept so dark that it takes a Seeing Eye dog to get you safely to a table if you don't want to find yourself sitting on someone's lap, and a flashlight to read your menu. It suited me fine and I had gone there often.

It was a little after one o'clock when I parked the Volkswagen in a patch of shade behind the restaurant and went in to find my favorite corner table unoccupied. This, I had learned, was an excellent vantage point from which, once my eyes were adjusted to the dusky interior, I could see anyone who came in.

I ordered a frosted daiquiri and sipped it, savoring the icy tartness. Slowly the tensions that made knots in the back of my neck began to relax. For one blindingly happy moment I had caught a glimpse of Will. He was all right and he was somewhere near me, watching over me. Soon the nightmare would be over and he could come for me. Perhaps even tomorrow.

By midafternoon I had found the shopping center near my new address and put in enough supplies to enable me to get my own meals for a few days. It was the unexpected encounter with some slight acquaintance or the startled recognition of someone who had seen the snapshot that could be disastrous. I avoided places where I had been accustomed to going, places where friends were apt to be found, but I couldn't, after all, be invisible. As I had told the young manager, I was no actress. There was always the moment of complete self-betrayal before I issued my denial and scuttled away.

As a result I had learned to go out as rarely as possible. With dark glasses, which are practically ubiquitous in southern California, and a blond wig that was not my kind of blond, with sloppy long culottes, bright-tinted blouses, and open sandals, I was so unlike my normal self that I was always taken aback when I was recognized as Helen Gates, the woman who was suspected of having murdered her husband.

The search for me would have been more intense during the six months that followed Will's disappearance and mine, if it had not been for three factors. For one thing there was no trace of Will's body. For another, it was his habit, familiar to everyone who knew him except his wife, to go away without explanation for weeks at a time. The third and clinching factor was that only Will and I knew that under some flimsy veiling in the top of my leather hatbox there were neat packages of currency amounting to almost eighty thousand dollars.

There were still days when I could not believe that this was happening to me, that I was hiding from a man who wanted to kill me, that I was wanted by the police for murder, and that I was concealing a small fortune in stolen money. I had never encountered anything unconventional, let alone criminal, in the first twenty-two years of my life. After a decorous and rigidly disciplined childhood I had spent a few years at an austere girl's school in Switzerland, where most of the pupils were either orphaned like myself or the children of divorced parents. I had been deeply impressed by the headmistress, a woman driven by a grim determination to sacrifice herself for others, no matter how strenuously they might resist. She was the woman who is always right and she made short work of the protests of people who thought they knew what was good for them.

It was because of her influence that I had come back to California to give my all to welfare work. But it was because of some lurking common sense that I began to doubt the essential rightness of my ideas and to yield to those of others.

For three years I was engaged in discovering the infinite number of ways in which people suffer through no fault of their own or the almost equally infinite number of ways in which people attempt to make unscrupulous use of their government, its funds, and its services. Human want and human greed. I met them both every day and found them equally depressing. So there had been little lighthearted gaiety in my life up to the time when I met Will Gates. I don't mean that I had been unhappy, just too sober and solemn and rather dull.

It was characteristic of Will that I met him because he came to the welfare agency to rescue one of my young clients, a boy who at seventeen had already begun to acquire a fairly impressive police record. Will wanted to give him a second chance. I had never met anyone like Will, with his flaming red hair, his joyous gusts of laughter, and his unruffled sweetness of nature. He was like a fresh breeze blowing through the stale air and the atmosphere of defeat or belligerence in the welfare agency.

After that first encounter Will and I met every single day until we were married six weeks later. He taught me all I knew about first-hand living and how to laugh and how to love. During those three months of our marriage I had fallen more and more deeply in love with him and he with me. There was no mistake about that and there was no shadow on our happiness except that Will was feckless and took no heed of tomorrow. Almost every day he brought me extravagant flowers. To celebrate the first month of our marriage, he turned in his old Ford and got a magnificent Cadillac. He rarely come home without some lovely gift: a jeweled pin or a pair of earrings or some exquisite negligee that had caught his fancy in a store window.

He brushed aside my protests. "I have a beautiful wife and she should have beautiful things."

He was, his boss, John Crothers, told me, the most brilliant salesman he had ever had. He could break down the strongest sales resistance. "He's a living wonder, Mrs. Gates," Crothers said. "With two men like Will I could have the most successful agency in the West. But there aren't two salesmen like him. He's *sui generis*."

I learned that if I protested too much about Will's extravagance I simply dimmed his gaiety and his delight in lavishing presents on me. The wolf wasn't anywhere near our door, he assured me. Why cloud the sunny days by worrying about the rainy ones? Was that sensible? I thought it was. But in the long run I stopped trying to change him. All I accomplished by my nagging was to make him restive and irritable, and it was for his gaiety as much as anything that I loved him. After I gave up my futile attempts to reform Will, things went smoothly with us.

The only other factor to threaten our happiness was Will's loyalty to his friend Harry Fitzhugh. I abandoned my attempt to balance our budget without too much protest, but Fitz's malignant influence on my husband I continued to fight.

"We've been friends all our lives," Will said. "He's

the closest thing I ever had to a kid brother. I'm not going to turn my back on him now, darling."

"I don't want you to do that, but I don't see why he has to come here so often. He drops in as though he owned the place."

"I suppose he feels that he does, in a way. We've always shared things."

"Does he have to share our apartment?" I disliked women who tried to break up their husbands' old friendships, and here I was doing it myself. I couldn't seem to help it.

Will didn't argue. He hated arguments and wanted everything to be smooth. He just laughed at me. "You're jealous, Helen."

That was too close for comfort, because there was a great deal of truth in it. I hated Fitz's influence; I resented his domination of Will; and I didn't like the man anyhow. Will said it was because I wasn't Fitz's type and he didn't pay me enough attention. What Fitz's type in women was I had no idea, as he had never brought a girl to our apartment, but I certainly wasn't it. He had not even tried to conceal his dismay when Will introduced us after our sudden marriage. He was aghast, rocked off his feet. But even his obvious dislike of me did not prevent him from continuing to treat our apartment as though it was his own, and certainly with no encouragement from me.

All this sounds as though Harry Fitzhugh was a rough sort of character. Nothing could be farther from the truth. He was somewhat under medium height, a good-looking young man of twenty-five with attractive manners, except where I was concerned. He might as well have shouted aloud his disapproval of me. Will told me that Fitz belonged to one of the most distinguished and aristocratic families in the South, which impressed him because his own father had been a clerk in a midwestern store and Will was surprisingly diffident about his background.

At this point Fitz could have had all the charm in

the world and it would not have weighed in his favor. Not with me. Because it was on his account that, after those three ecstatic months of marriage, I was a woman wanted by the police for questioning in regard to the strange disappearance of her husband whom, they suspected, I had murdered.

It is small wonder that I hated Harry Fitzhugh.

TWO

That last week Will had been nervous, starting at unexpected sounds, chain-smoking, and biting his nails, a habit he had almost conquered except when he was overtired. For the first time since our marriage there were hours at a time when I realized that he had forgotten my existence. He was sleeping badly. Usually hard to awaken in the morning, I had found him several times in the living room, fully dressed, an overflowing ashtray beside him by the time I got up.

For a couple of days I said nothing because I felt that he would confide in me if he wanted to. If he chose not to I had no right to invade his privacy. And in the long run he explained that he was worried about Fitz. He was afraid that the poor guy was headed for trouble. I couldn't have cared less except for the fact that Will was upset.

Then, on that last day, Will came home in midmorning, carrying a big suitcase. He was white and shaken.

Fitz, he told me, was in awful trouble. His father was desperately ill and headed for a dangerous and expensive operation, to be followed by a long period of intensive care in a nursing home, with round-the-clock nurses. He had tried in every possible way to raise the money. Then, with time running out, if he was to save his father, he had held up the messenger who delivered the monthly payroll to the company where he worked. Will indicated helplessly the suitcase.

"You mean," I gasped, "that's it? That's the stolen money?"

Will nodded. "Fitz called me at the agency this morning and asked me to go down to his place. He was just about out of his mind."

"So are you," I told him grimly, "if you let him involve you in this awful thing."

"There is no one else he could go to," Will reminded me. "And that's not all. That's not even the worst."

I braced myself but I wasn't prepared for the blow when it came. There had been half a dozen big payroll robberies in the past year and a half and unpublicized steps had been taken by a number of companies to end the situation. For instance, the messenger who usually delivered the payroll for Fitz's company had been replaced by an armed guard. When the latter had drawn his gun, Fitz had lost his head, panicked, and shot him dead. He had rushed back to his apartment with the suitcase containing the payroll money and discovered when he examined it that his company had baited a trap in case a hold-up should prove to be successful. The money had been marked so that it could be spotted as soon as it was put into circulation. Obviously all banks had been alerted. So Fitz realized that the risk he had taken had been for nothing.

"And a man is dead," I reminded Will hotly. "I won't have you involved in this. I won't. I won't!"

My voice had risen. Will pulled me into his arms. I could feel him shaking, feel the pounding of his heart. "Listen, darling, the poor devil didn't mean to do it. He just got scared and lost his head. We can't change what happened to the guard. Oh, God, I wish we could!"

But even the genuine torment in his voice did not alter my attitude. "What do you intend to do with that money, Will? Why did you bring it here instead of restoring it to the company where it belongs?"

"I've got to protect Fitz from himself. Can't you see that? Right now he isn't thinking straight. He still believes that he can save his father and pay for the operation by using that marked money. I tried my damnedest to make him understand that as soon as any of it turns up he'll be arrested not just for theft but for murder. The shock would kill his father and Fitz would end in the gas chamber! Fitz! But he won't listen to me. So I knocked him down and took the money away from him."

"But why bring it here?"

"I had to." Will had sunk down on the couch as though he could not stand. "I've known for a week that Fitz was in bad trouble and planning something, but he wouldn't tell me until it was a *fait accompli*. Too late, of course. I didn't know what to do, darling, except that I couldn't leave the money with Fitz."

"Well?" This time I was fighting all the way. "It's stolen money, Will. It has to go back."

Again Will made one of those oddly helpless gestures that were so uncharacteristic of him. "He—I told you he isn't thinking straight. When I took the money away from him, he swore that if I turned it in he would kill you. He—means it, Helen. It's the one threat that he knew would work because you are the one human being who has ever been important to me; more important than Fitz, I mean. Nothing I could say mattered. It's hell, love. It's absolute hell. I can't destroy Fitz, but I can't let him destroy you." Will ran his hands over his face and head as though he were too weary to cope with the situation.

"But, Will, love—"

"I've been trying to think what would be best for everyone and I believe I've worked it out. The main thing is that you've got to disappear so Fitz can't touch you."

I stared at him in utter disbelief. "You are mad as a hatter," I said at last flatly. "I never heard of such a preposterous idea. Fitz threatens to kill me so, instead of having him locked up where he belongs, you want me to go into hiding. I absolutely refuse."

"But, Helen." Will held out his hand to me, partly for comfort, partly seeking my support.

Childishly I put both my hands behind my back so I wouldn't touch him. "Fitz is a murderer. You said so yourself."

"Can't you see, darling, that's why he is a genuine threat to you? I can't betray a man who is like a brother; I can't let him hurt my wife. The danger is very real. This is just plain hell, but it's only temporary, Helen. Oh, God, don't fail me now."

"What do you want me to do?"

Will's moods were always mercurial. He brightened at once at the indication that I was willing at least to listen to his plan. "You'll get lost for a few days or weeks at the outside. Fitz's father can't last that long and after his death the money won't be needed and Fitz will come to his senses. I'll act as a sort of red herring and leave tracks so he will hunt me down and take the heat off you. And we'll arrange to have people believe that I never came home after leaving Fitz, and that the money is therefore still in my possession."

He wasn't shaking so much now and his heart and breathing had steadied. He got up again and held me tightly, trying as best he could to beat down my resistance and my horrified determination to have no part in the whole unspeakable situation.

"Do you want us to go separate ways? Is this the end of our marriage, Will?"

"We aren't breaking up! Just for a short time we'll keep apart so Fitz can't find you. You'll be safe and he'll be safe. I can't—have you ever read a description of a man dying in the gas chamber? I can't do that to Fitz!"

"What about the money?" I touched the heavy suitcase with the toe of my shoe.

"Good God!" Will was horrified. "You don't think I want it, do you? I'll leave it with you where Fitz can't find it, and as soon as it is safe, we'll put it back where it belongs. But we've got to hold on to it now. If we return it, the story will break in the news, and Fitz will retaliate by killing you."

"No!" I shouted. "No! I won't! You can't! I won't! No!" I thrust Will back so violently that he lost his balance and staggered against a table, setting a tall metal vase to rocking so violently that it fell on the floor with a crash, and the magnificent American Beauty roses he had brought me the day before lay scattered on the rug.

"Quiet," he warned me. "Everyone in the building will hear you. It's just for a little while, my darling: so an old man can die in peace and Fitz can start thinking straight. Because if he were to injure you in any way, I think I could kill him myself."

"Look, Will," and I tried to be reasonable, to be quiet, to make him see what he was doing, what he was involving us both in, "you don't know what you are doing. You're making yourself an accessory. Can't you see that? There's no moratorium on murder. This is a criminal thing you are trying to become a part of."

"It's for you, Helen, as well as for Fitz. Try to understand."

"You're asking me to become an accessory too, aren't you? Can that possibly be what you want?"

"It's up to you," he said slowly. "My way gives us a chance—all of us. Sooner or later I can talk sense into Fitz, maybe help him get out of the country, work things out for us, for you and me. Your way—there's no chance at all. Fitz will track you down to get even with me. He'll end in the gas chamber. I—God knows. Maybe prison because I've tried to shield him. Is that what you think right?"

"There isn't any right in this setup."

But in the long run, bitterly as I resented the whole situation, I capitulated, as he had known all along I would, and agreed to do as Will wanted. The humiliating fact was that I was still convinced that I was right, but I reminded myself of the headmistress who had been equally sure. Anyhow, I was putty in Will's hands because I loved him. Even in my capitulation, though, I hated Fitz for having done this to me.

Perhaps Will had been right and I was jealous of his loyalty to Harry Fitzhugh. Perhaps Will could not betray his friend or let him risk his freedom and his life by spending the marked money. Perhaps my ideas of justice were archaic, an eye for an eye, and punishing the criminal. According to the new school there were no criminals, only sick people who were not responsible for their actions. I wished to God that I knew what to believe and what to do.

When I was quiet enough to make plans, Will said, "I figure we've got less than twenty-four hours' leeway. I tied Fitz up so he can't possibly free himself. You're safe until his cleaning woman comes at noon tomorrow. You probably ought to change your appearance a bit if you are not to be recognized. You know how people are always asking if you are a younger sister of Princess Grace. That same scrubbed look and the lovely simplicity that gives you a kind of distinction, or elegance, or whatever it should be called. You should make yourself—oh, fancier, more flamboyant. And we are going to need money." As I glanced doubtfully at the suitcase, he said, "Not that! We don't touch that, whatever we do. But I guess," he added with a rueful look, "this is one of the times when it would have paid off to follow your advice and put away a part of my earnings."

"I have about ten thousand dollars in savings and two or three thousand in my checking account. Everything else is in stocks and bonds and I couldn't get at it in a hurry."

"That should be more than enough, though I suppose we ought to allow for emergencies."

In the afternoon I took the Cadillac and went to my bank, where I closed out both my checking and savings accounts. Then I went to half a dozen banks where I was unknown and got traveler's checks at each one, but in small enough amounts so as not to attract attention. Three thousand dollars seemed to be enough for me, and I got the checks in my maiden name, as Will had suggested. The rest of the money, about ten thousand, was in bills of fairly large denominations, but even so, it made an awfully thick package, but Will would find some way to handle it.

At a large department store where mobs of women were trying on wigs, I bought one, selected garish slacks and culottes and skirts and sandals and a new and flamboyant kind of make-up. None of it seemed real. I felt rather as though I were preparing for a masquerade and not to go into hiding from a man who threatened to kill me.

When I got back to the apartment, I was brought up with a start to the realities of the situation and a grim reminder that we were not playing a game. I turned my key in the lock, but the door did not open. The bolt had been shoved on.

"Will," I called and I heard him draw the bolt and open the door.

"I wasn't taking any chances while this damned money is still in the place," he said. Now that the initial shock of the situation was over, I saw how deeply shaken he had been. His freckles stood out on his colorless face and his red hair stood on end from running his finger through it. I couldn't bear to have him suffer so. His wife and his oldest friend. It was hell for him.

I stood on tiptoe to kiss him. "It's going to be all right, love. We'll make it all right."

He held me in a crushing embrace. "How did I ever have the luck to find you, and to win you after I found you?"

He had me try on the clothes and make-up and wig and laughed like a boy when he saw the transformation. Temporarily he seemed to have forgotten that he had involved us both in theft and murder. With his customary resilience he had risen like a phoenix from the morning's shock and he talked gaily, settling the details as though this were to be some lighthearted adventure; arranging code names so we could get in touch with each other in an emergency.

That night any idea that this was a game had to be abandoned when we turned on the television set and heard the news. The story of the payroll robbery and the slain guard got a lot of attention. There was a special human interest angle because the guard, after twenty-five years with the agency that provided men to protect payrolls, as well as the transportation of furs and jewelry and valuable art works, had been on the verge of retirement.

There was no mention of the fact that the money had been in marked currency. Clearly the police were not telling all they knew.

We talked late and I fell asleep at last in the warm circle of Will's arms, my head on his breast. In the end I had put aside my hostility because Will was the one who needed consolation and support. He had been faced with a dilemma that involved the two people he loved most in the world and he had met it in the only way he could if one of us was not to be destroyed.

"Remember," Will said as I was falling asleep, "we must get up early and leave the apartment as soon as possible, so we'll be safely out of the way before Fitz gets here."

When I awakened next morning, Will was not beside me. He wasn't in the apartment. He had left behind everything except the clothes he was wearing, even his toothbrush and shaving kit. The night before, the stolen money had been stowed away in my big black-leather hatbox, with a piece of filmy veiling over the top and a black thread stretched across it so we would know if it was disturbed.

There was a letter propped on the living room table, the first of all the letters. Will was one of the curious products of our educational system. He was highly intelligent and he had a well-informed mind, but he read rather slowly and his handwriting was practically undecipherable. With the exception of his signature he invariably printed instead of using script.

"Darling," the note said, "I couldn't bear to say good-by, even for so short a time. Get out as soon as you have packed. Remember that I'll be keeping an eye on you. When it is safe for you, I'll come. I'll love you forever. Will."

There was no vestige of the sense of adventure now. Will had gone out of reach and I could not turn back from the course I had agreed upon. When I had had some coffee, I packed hastily, dressed in the trashy clothes, made up my face, and put on the wig, which was combed in a beehive and teased until it looked about a foot high. Then I shoved on dark glasses.

I stood looking around the rooms where Will and I had been so happy, wondering bleakly whether we could ever recapture that happiness. I had kept the apartment spotless and shining. Now the bedroom was cluttered with the disorder Will always managed to create around him. The vase he had knocked over when I pushed him lay on the floor in a pool of water and the flowers had already withered.

"Leave them," Will had said. "When Fitz comes looking for you and sees this mess, he will know for sure that we cleared out. He'll grasp the fact that I mean business."

I picked up one of the roses and broke off the stem and put the blossom gently in my billfold. Then I remembered my wedding ring, slipped it off and dropped it into a zipper pocket in my purse.

I went out of the building, hoping I would not meet anyone while I looked so incredibly unlike myself. Will had left the Cadillac in its usual slot. That was part of his plan, too. Oddly enough, that impressed me more than anything else with the gravity of the situation as Will saw it. He loved the car and it would be difficult for him to give it up, even for a short time.

Anyhow, like most Americans, he had practically forgotten how to walk. He would take out the car even if he was going only a couple of blocks.

Following his instructions, I walked for what seemed to be miles before I found a used-car lot and paid four hundred dollars in traveler's checks, made out in my maiden name of Helen Brown because I still had my old driving license in that name. I bought an old Volkswagen, which I parked on the street a block away from the apartment while I went in to get my suitcases. I lifted the heavy leather hatbox off a shelf as warily as though it were a cobra. Just as I was about to leave, the telephone rang.

"Hello, beautiful! Is Will there?" The familiar cheerful voice was that of John Crothers, manager of the automobile agency where Will worked. After seeing him a few times I had made excuses to avoid attending his parties. He was the kind of man who automatically makes passes at any woman he meets, so it didn't mean anything personal, but I knew Will would be angry if he noticed it and I didn't want him to have any hostility toward his boss because of his wife.

"Why, no!" I hoped I sounded surprised. "He didn't come home last night because he had several prospects he could see only in the evening and he expected to be awfully late, so it was simpler to go to a hotel."

"Which hotel? Do you know?"

I hesitated as though searching my memory. "No," I said firmly, "I don't remember. But you'll probably see him any minute now."

Crothers laughed. "He most probably stopped off on the way to make another sale. That husband of yours is terrific, in case you don't know it. A customer is here waiting to buy two cars. Will made the sale the other day. Just paper work now. Well, I'll ask the guy to wait. Even Will isn't going to forget a deal like this." With another laugh he hung up.

The anger that had been submerged during the

night in Will's arms came surging back. Because of Fitz, Will had gone off into the blue, sacrificing his job and the big commission he would have earned this morning. Because of Fitz I was going into hiding, the reluctant custodian of eighty thousand dollars in stolen money. Because of Fitz a man lay dead, a man who had simply been doing his job when Fitz shot him down.

There was only one point on which I had decided to follow my own judgment and I hadn't dared to tell Will for fear he would dissuade me. The more I thought of having the stolen money in my possession, the more it had terrified me. I had made and discarded half a dozen plans for keeping it safe and finally decided on one possibility. I wasn't proud of myself for intending to make use of my friends, but I didn't know what else to do. Where everything seemed wrong, I could only settle on what seemed the least wrong.

The Hepburns were about the only people in southern California with whom I had kept in close touch. After my marriage I had drifted away from most of my old friends. They all liked Will, of course, but they didn't have much in common and he was unexpectedly sensitive about his different background and inclined to see snubs where none were intended. But the Hepburns had been old friends of my parents. They had visited me when I was at school abroad and remembered my birthday and had me spend my vacations with them. Their house was a huge and beautiful Spanish structure set in spacious grounds, dramatically landscaped, and their goodness was such that even Will could not imagine that he was being slighted. In fact, he loved to go there, naïvely impressed by the magnificence of the house, its furnishings, and the number of its servants.

"Someday, love, we'll have a place like this," he assured me.

I could have told him that I might have had several

such houses if that had been all I wanted, but I didn't. He would only have been distressed, feeling that he did not measure up.

When I left the apartment, I stood for a moment searching the busy street for Fitz, wondering if he was lurking near me. Fitz who would punish Will for removing the marked money by killing me. Fitz who had already killed. From that minute on there was never to be a time when I went out of doors without looking for Fitz, when my heart did not jolt at the sight of some man on the street who walked like him. No one can know what it is like to hide from a killer unless he has experienced it, though in time even fear becomes part of a familiar pattern.

From the apartment I drove straight to the Hepburn house and it was like moving from one world to another; in a sense, that was just what it was. Our apartment was on a heavily traveled main thoroughfare with endless traffic and the rumble of heavy trucking and the eerie wail of sirens, presaging disaster. But the Hepburns lived in a section with curving roads that shut its houses away in almost inviolable privacy.

The house was hidden from the road by a twelve-foot hedge. As usual the iron gates stood open and I followed the winding road up to the house. There were vivid flowers on either side of the driveway and the lawn was an emerald green. Deodars scattered over the vast grounds, imported many years before from India, and the magnificent huge gnarled oaks that are such a delight in California, provided shady spots on the grounds.

The house had been built around an open court so it seemed far bigger even than it actually was. I lifted the hatbox out of the Volkswagen and went to the door. The butler looked me over with trained eyes. Apparently he took the hatbox for a sample case and supposed I was a house-to-house canvasser.

"Mrs. Hepburn is not at home."

I laughed, though I'd have been at a loss to say

what was funny about the situation. "Don't you know me, Wilkins?"

His jaw dropped. "Miss Brown! I mean Mrs. Gates. I—" He left me and returned almost at once. "Will you come back to the morning room, please?"

Mrs. Hepburn was a massive woman, tall and heavy, with rather forbidding manners to those who did not know her. She was regarded as a holy terror by people who did not know her well and she could be formidable in dealing with anyone foolhardy enough to attempt to cheat her or make unscrupulous use of her. She was so secure socially that she did not concern herself with fashion, regarding the slavish admiration of Parisian couturiers as a vulgarity for the use of people with more money than judgment. From some obscure source she still managed to get highboned net collars and jet jewelry and she wore a pince-nez that hooked over a gold pin in her shelf-like bosom.

She was typing menus with one finger on a bright-colored little portable typewriter and she turned to smile at me, the smile fading when she saw the wig, the make-up, and the sleazy clothing.

"Helen!" she said in a tone of bewilderment.

"I know how horrible I look, but there's a reason for it. I can't explain now."

Shrewd eyes raked my face and then rested on the hatbox. "I hope you've come for a few days' visit," she said casually. "I was telling Burton last night I felt guilty having that wonderful pool and no young people to enjoy it. Anyhow, we don't see enough of you. The guest suite that overlooks the patio is absolutely quiet, my dear; you couldn't hear a sound of traffic there."

I remembered how shocked she had been on her only visit to the apartment to discover how noisy it was. I went over to hug her. I might have known that, even looking as vulgar as I did, she would accept me without hesitation and without question. For a moment the temptation to stay there or at least to tell her the whole story seemed too strong to withstand. But I couldn't involve her in this horrible business, at least not beyond the limits I had set myself.

"I wish I could stay," I told her, "but it's out of the question."

"There's room for your husband too, of course." She was still casual and noncommittal.

"He'd love it but he's—that is, Will has gone out of town on business for the agency. He's a car salesman, you know." It sounded flat and unconvincing. "But there is something. The thing is—well, may I leave this hatbox with you for safekeeping? Once Mr. Hepburn showed me that big vault in the basement and I wondered if there would be room for this."

Her gaze was direct now. "Are you in trouble, Helen?"

"I'm not sure," I answered.

"Well, I'm glad you had sense enough to come to us. Leave your hatbox, my dear, and we'll look after it for you."

"Thank you." To my embarrassment I had to struggle not to cry. This kindly world was the one I was accustomed to, not the upside-down world into which Harry Fitzhugh had propelled me.

"Your rooms will always be waiting for you, my dear." She nodded to her housekeeper, who stood hesitating in the doorway. "Come in. I've nearly finished the menus. And remember to impress on the cook that Mr. Hepburn does not like his food too highly seasoned. It does not agree with him."

She smiled at me and waved her hand in dismissal, as though she had not seen how upset I was and how close to tears. But with her foot she shoved the hatbox under her desk and out of the housekeeper's range of vision. Wilkins was not in the hall, so I let myself out. Only Mrs. Hepburn and I knew that I had arrived carrying a hatbox and that I had left without it.

THREE

Late that afternoon I paid a month's rent on an apartment under my maiden name of Helen Brown. I was surprised to discover how easy it was. The renting agent took no interest in me and asked no embarrassing questions. He did not require any credentials. The transients who took furnished apartments without a lease moved in and out so frequently that he was interested in nothing but the rent.

The following morning there was a letter under my door when I got up. "You're doing fine, darling. I'm near you. Don't worry. It won't be long. Dearest love, Will."

That night there was an interview on television with the dead guard's widow, a woman so dazed by pain and loss that I could not bear to look at her. It seemed indecent to spy on her grief.

"All these years," she said, "and not a single shot. I'd forgotten a long time ago to worry about Joe. And we were going to get a place on the beach where he could go fishing. He's been buying fishing tackle for months and he didn't even get a chance to use it. I wish he could have gone fishing just once; he'd looked forward to it so hard. He would never have hurt anyone. In all these years he never fired a shot except at a target, so why did it happen? Why? He didn't need to be killed."

The reporter also interviewed an angry public official who was working on crime prevention. Payroll thefts, he declared, were increasing, and proper precautions were not being taken by enough companies. It was easy for a corrupt employee to tip off a thief as to the time the payroll was to be delivered and how the delivery was made. Large businesses with heavy payrolls were being urged either to pay by check or to adopt stricter security measures.

That meant, didn't it, that Fitz had betrayed himself in some way and the police were on his track. I prayed that he would be captured soon and that Will and I could go back to our normal lives. But, though I never failed to listen to the news from that time on, there was no further word about the payroll robbery. It just dropped out, like so many stories. Often, weeks or months later, one remembers and asks, "Whatever happened to him? Or how did that story end?"

On the following day Will's disappearance broke in the news in the most unexpected way. Will Gates, an automobile salesman, had sold two high-priced cars to a single customer and then he had not appeared to close the sale. John Crothers, manager of the agency in which he worked and active in the Chamber of Commerce, had telephoned Mrs. Gates, who told him that her husband had not come home the night before. He had had to see several prospects during the evening and he expected to spend the night at a hotel because he would be too late to get home. She did not remember which hotel he planned to stay at.

When Gates failed to report at the agency two days in succession, Mr. Crothers telephoned repeatedly to his apartment, but there was no answer. Occasionally in the past Mr. Gates had gone on vacation without warning, but usually he got in touch with the agency, and he had never taken off leaving unfinished business behind.

In some alarm Mr. Crothers went to the building in which Will Gates had an apartment and saw the superintendent. The latter told him that the Gates Cadillac was parked in its usual slot, so he had assumed that both Mr. and Mrs. Gates were at home. He also stated that the day before Gates had failed to show up at the agency he and his wife had a noisy quarrel in midmorning. She had been heard shouting at him and they seemed to be knocking things around. Later that afternoon Mrs. Gates had been observed returning to the apartment, driving the Cadillac, which had not been moved since then. Neither Mr. nor Mrs. Gates had been seen after that.

The superintendent admitted Mr. Crothers, now seriously alarmed, to the apartment, which was unoccupied. Mr. Gates' suits, shoes, and underwear had been left behind, as well as his toothbrush and his razor. All of Mrs. Gates' clothing was gone and there were indications of hasty packing. Indeed the apartment was in a state of considerable confusion though, when the superintendent had had the occasion to enter it in the past, it had always been unusually orderly.

A heavy metal vase lay on the floor in the living room and beautiful long-stemmed roses had withered on the rug, which was soaked with water from the vase.

Everything about that broadcast, even hedged about as it was with "appeared to be," "alleged," "might have been," implied that Will had been killed and his body disposed of and I had cleared out with all my belongings. As I could hardly have accomplished all this by myself, I must presumably have had masculine assistance.

"Mr. Crothers," the commentator went on to say, "described Mrs. Gates as a young and very beautiful woman. Neighbors, when questioned, agreed that there had been a violent quarrel, the only one anyone had ever heard, as Mr. Gates was a bridegroom and a devoted husband, bringing his wife flowers almost every day. The couple entertained rarely but there was a young man who visited them frequently, coming at all hours as though he was quite at home."

The description that followed was a surprisingly accurate one of Fitz. Of all unexpected turns, this was the most surprising. Will had persuaded me to go into hiding to protect me from Fitz, and now Fitz and I were suspected of having connived at Will's murder. I wondered what Fitz was thinking when he heard that broadcast. He had always hated me and resented my marriage. To be suspected of being my lover and my accomplice in killing Will would be a bitter thing for him and there was, ironically, no way in which he could clear himself of suspicion unless he could produce Will and me, and both of us had gone into hiding to escape him. There was a kind of poetic justice in Fitz finding himself in this Gilbertian situation.

What, I wondered, would the Hepburns be thinking of me? They had known me all my life and they must have been aware that I was infatuated with my husband. They would not for a minute believe that I had been unfaithful to him, let alone that I was capable of murder. But there was my ill-timed and ill-considered visit to Mrs. Hepburn, my refusal to explain what the trouble was, my vulgar masquerade, and my gratuitous lie that Will had gone out of town on business. At best they would know me to be a liar. And they must, because of their genuine fondness for me, be half wild with anxiety about my inexplicable disappearance. They must be asking themselves about my incomprehensible behavior and the meaning of the hatbox, and the vanishing of Will, who had left behind all his belongings, even his new car.

I was terribly tempted to call Mrs. Hepburn and to reassure her, to say that Will and I were both alive and well. But when I tried to think of how much it would be safe to tell her, I quailed. One thing I was aware of: fond as the Hepburns were of me, neither of them would feel justified in helping me to shield a murderer or to conceal stolen money. They would feel obliged to report the whole situation to the police, which meant that Harry Fitzhugh would be arrested and probably sentenced to die in the gas chamber. And Will would never forgive me for betraying his friend.

For about a week the events in which I was involved dropped from the news, except for a poignant account of the funeral of the guard whom Fitz had shot, and a picture of his widow, dry-eyed and slack-mouthed, standing alone beside his grave, apparently unaware of the drenching rain.

Then, just when I had begun to think that nothing more would happen, I was startled to look at the television screen one evening and see a picture of me. At first I could not imagine where it had come from as I had never seen it before. Then I recalled that Fitz had snapped me the day Will introduced us. It was an excellent likeness of Helen Gates, but I could see little resemblance between the woman in the picture and the woman I was now. My clothes were always simple and I wore little make-up. My hair was brushed back smoothly into a thick roll at the back. What did puzzle me was how the picture had got into the hands of the police, as only Fitz had one.

The story that accompanied the picture was disturbing. The search for Will Gates, missing car salesman, and his bride of three months, was being intensified. The police had learned that on the day before her disappearance Mrs. Gates had closed out both her checking and her savings accounts, which indicated that her disappearance had been premeditated. A small running account of several hundred dollars in the name of Will Gates had not been drawn upon.

Next day there was a second picture of me, a cabinet portrait in profile I had had made for Will. He had loved it, but he had left it behind as he had left all his belongings, and the police, presumably, had taken it from our apartment. I winced at the thought of the apartment I had planned with such joy being invaded by the police, and our belongings turned over by alien hands.

With that second picture there was the statement: "Have you seen this woman? Helen Gates, aged twenty-three, height five feet five, weight 118 pounds, blond hair, blue eyes. Wanted for questioning in regard to the disappearance of her husband, Will Gates. Anyone having any information as to her whereabouts will please report to the police."

I stared at it in disbelief. This couldn't be happening to me. A woman wanted by the police. Will couldn't let it happen. Anything would be better than this. It seemed to me I had no choice now except to surrender to the police.

But next morning Will brushed past me in a supermarket and his hand closed swiftly over mine. "Don't give up the ship," he whispered. Before I could get a close look at him, he had gone through a turnstile, but at least I had recognized the sports jacket he was wearing and the oddly shaped dark glasses. His red hair was concealed by a cap. Because I was wedged between my grocery cart and a heavy woman who blocked the aisle behind me, I could not extricate myself for several minutes. By the time I had got free, he was out of sight.

That day I cried with frustration. As the situation worsened, I needed Will so terribly that I nearly shouted his name as I ran through the parking lot, trying to find him, but he was gone. I reminded myself that he was keeping out of my way for my own protection, but it did not help. He must know how terrible it was to be wanted by the police. He must know how anxious I was about him. This persistent silence wasn't like him. Not a bit like him.

A day or so later I carelessly removed my dark glasses to read a price tag and the clerk who was waiting on me gasped. "My God, you look like that woman. You know, the one who killed her husband."

I managed a laugh though my face felt stiff. "Good heavens, I'd better look out."

"It sure gave me a start. I guess I hadn't seen your eyes before or looked at you in profile, though I remember you come in here regular."

That was the first time I moved.

Six months later I had come to accept the new pattern of my life. Though I had never been gregarious, I had never before been completely alone. Now I learned to spend afternoons at the movies where I would not be recognized in a darkened theater, and in the evenings I read paperback books. I did not dare use the public libary because I was known to the staff and I tried to keep out of well-lighted stores unless I could have the anonymity of the mob. Night after night I lay awake, wondering where Will was and what he was doing. Sometimes I wanted him so badly that I nearly cried out. Sometimes I thought I hated him as I hated Fitz for putting me in this intolerable situation.

But little by little, almost without being aware of it, I stopped expecting Will to come back. I no longer looked along every street seeking for him. It was as though he was gradually fading into the distance, out of sight, out of reach. Another day, I told myself, and I would retrieve the hatbox and restore the money to the people to whom it belonged, even if it meant that Fitz would carry out his threat. But I kept on waiting just one more day. Hope dies hard.

FOUR

The morning after I had moved into the little pink cottage I found myself singing as I washed the breakfast dishes and made my bed. I had seen Will, if only for a moment and at a distance. He was not far away; he knew how to find me even if I could not reach him. The nightmare of the past weeks faded like fog dissipating under a hot sun, and the future seemed bright with promise.

Because I was the only tenant in the cottages, I risked going into the pool. At last I climbed out to turn over on my face on a plastic lounge with the sun hot and healing on my back. I had not put on my cheap make-up and I hadn't bothered with a cap, so I let the sun dry my hair, which is thick and long, hanging below my waist. Hair as heavy as mine is a nuisance to deal with and I'd been tempted to cut it, but Will loved it and begged me not to. He called it liquid sunshine and he liked to take out the pins and let it fall. It was better not to think of that now that he could not see it.

I was half asleep when I heard voices and sat up with a start. The young manager was coming toward me at her usual quick walk, followed by a girl who wore an extreme mini skirt. Black hair had been teased until it resembled a bird's nest.

For a moment the manager did not recognize me. I could see her surprised expression before she called cheerfully, "Hi, there! You ought to watch out just at first, Miss Brown. You're so fair that you are apt to burn easily. This is Miss Wilson, your new neighbor. She has taken the yellow cottage."

I smiled. "I hope you'll enjoy it."

"Thanks. I expect to." She summed me up as coolly as though I was something displayed on a marked-down counter.

"We're going to have some coffee. Do come along with us," the manager said hospitably. "It will help you girls get acquainted."

Reluctantly, and because it was easier to go along than to think of some excuse when I was obviously doing nothing but enjoying a sun bath. I pulled my terry cloth cape over my shoulders and wrapped my damp hair in a towel, which I twisted around my head.

"What gorgeous hair!" the manager said. "If it were mine, I'd wear it hanging like that so people could see it, instead of covering it with a wig."

"Still," Miss Wilson commented, "wigs are useful for a change, aren't they? Cover a multitude of sins."

I looked at her quickly, suspicious of some double meaning, but she was inspecting the pool. She bent over to test the temperature. She hadn't meant anything. I was getting to the point where I was always wondering about people's motives.

Like my cottage, the manager's apartment had a dining nook on one side of the living room, while the kitchen was separated from the room only by a wide counter along one side. An appetizing smell of baking permeated the room and the oven door was open, evidently cooling.

While Miss Wilson made out a check for a month's rent I played with the little boy, an enchanting child with dark blue eyes and an irresistible smile. He tried to climb out of his playpen, holding out his arms to me, his voice clamorous.

"May I take him?" I asked his mother.

"Sure. I never knew Johnny to want to go to any stranger before. You must have a way with children."

I picked him up and settled him on my lap, his sweet-smelling hair against my cheek. I can't remember ever before having a sensation like that of holding the small warm body against me.

Will and I had wanted to start a family, but he had said we'd put it off for a while. He wanted to have me to himself for the time being. It occurred to me now that unless I could be completely cleared of the suspicions against me, it would be unfair to have a child, a child who might someday, in turning over an old newspaper, see a picture of his mother marked, "This Woman Wanted."

"The coffee's ready and I just baked some dandy gingerbread," the manager said. "Do have some. I love having people drop in for morning coffee, don't you?" She poured coffee and brought the cups to the new tenant and me.

"Now this is real friendly," Miss Wilson said. "I didn't get your names. I'm bad that way."

"Our name is Mason," the manager said. "I'm Gillian Mason, but people mostly call me Jill. My husband's name is Jack. I think it's kind of cute."

"Jack and Jill. It's real cute," Miss Wilson agreed. "My name is Marilyn."

"Hi, Marilyn," Jill said breezily.

Will had impressed on me that I was not to get involved with anyone, but I saw that it would be difficult not to be on friendly and informal terms with anyone as open-hearted as Jill Mason.

Marilyn Wilson looked me over coolly, though I didn't understand how she could raise her lids, weighted down as they were by artificial lashes that looked an inch long. "I didn't get your name."

"Brown. Helen Brown."

"Are you working here?"

"No, I'm just a refugee from a New England winter."

"Nice if you can afford it. I'm looking out for something with a future in it, if you know what I mean.

There aren't enough men to go round, so a girl has to look after herself."

I felt that she was equipped to do it if anyone could. When Johnny turned to peer up at me, I laughed down at him, watching for his enchanting smile.

"Of course I work now and then," Marilyn Wilson went on. "My brother-in-law has a restaurant and I fill in at odd hours when he can't get help. It's not regular, but I like it in a way because it leaves me a lot of free time."

Jill passed gingerbread that was light as a feather and she seemed to be delighted when we praised it. There were dishes stacked in the sink and through an open door I saw an unmade bed.

"Aren't we interrupting your work?"

Jill curled up on the couch, obviously prepared to settle down for a leisurely and friendly chat. "Gosh, no. There's always time for housework, but I don't let it ride me. Enjoy yourself while you can. That's my motto. You can be sure the dishes will be waiting when there's nothing more interesting to do. Anyhow, there are some good television programs in the afternoon and I can watch them while I do the housework, and we've got a real good color set."

I thought uneasily that I ought to go. Hard as it seemed to relinquish that enchanting small boy, it would be safer for me to leave before I made any damaging admissions. Will had warned me to think twice before I answered any questions, no matter how harmless they might seem, but before I could get up, there was a shadow in the open doorway and Jill turned her head.

"Yes? You looking for me?"

"Are you the manager?"

"Yes, I am."

"I understand you have a furnished apartment for rent."

At the sound of a masculine voice Marilyn Wilson

brightened and fluttered those improbable lashes. I bent my head low over the little boy, trying to conceal my face.

"It's a cottage, actually. The apartments are all rented. Would you like to see one of the cottages?"

"Mm, that smells good," he said appreciatively.

"The gingerbread? I made it myself. Do have some coffee and gingerbread with us. Oh, these are two of your neighbors if you move in. Miss Wilson and Miss Brown."

"Now that's very nice of you." He came forward, smiled at the black-haired girl and murmured, "Miss Wilson." He turned to me. "Miss Brown," he said blandly.

I knew, even before I looked up, who he was; he drove a white Pontiac and yesterday he had addressed me as Mrs. Gates. Not the wildest coincidence could have brought him here the day after I moved in. He must have followed me.

"My name is Ronald Boyd," he said, as he pulled up a chair and lifted his coffee cup. His eyes brushed over my face, lingered on my legs, and went on to Marilyn, who was trying to attract his attention. "This is delicious," he declared when he had sampled the gingerbread. "It seems almost too good to be true to taste some real home cooking."

"The surest way to a man's heart," Marilyn said with a brittle laugh. "Is gingerbread your favorite food?"

"It is now. In a previous dull existence devoid of gingerbread I would have voted for popovers."

The telephone rang and Jill excused herself to answer it. Johnny, who had been sitting contentedly on my lap, became restless as soon as his mother moved away and he wriggled impatiently in my arms. When I set him down, he started after her with a staggering motion of a child who is just learning to walk, and lost his balance. I must have crossed the room in one long sidelong motion and I snatched him up before he could fall against that open oven door. I felt a searing pain along my arm.

Jill broke off her telephone conversation and came running. "Did you hurt yourself?"

"Better close that oven door," I said sharply.

She did so and then insisted on looking at my arm. Unfortunately the terry cloth cape had fallen open when I lunged for Johnny and there was an ugly red welt on my arm. With a little cry of distress she ran for a tube of ointment and applied it lavishly to the burn. Boyd took Johnny out of my arms and restored him to his playpen, where he watched, absorbed, while his mother doctored the burn.

"Maybe we'd better get you to a doctor," Jill said anxiously. "It looks awfully deep to me."

"Nonsense. It will be all right. Please don't bother."

"I'd be happy to run you over to the hospital," Boyd offered. "The emergency room could fix you up in no time."

Marilyn's eyes went from his face to mine.

"Thanks," I said curtly. "It isn't necessary."

Jill said, "I wish we had something stronger than coffee, but neither Jack nor I care much about drinking and it costs so much now that we settle for Cokes and maybe a beer on Saturday night."

"Coffee's fine and I really don't need a drink."

She had just refilled my cup when she turned to say, "Hi, there!"

A uniformed policeman was standing in the doorway. For a long moment I stared at him, coffee splashing on the rug as I dropped the cup.

FIVE

"This is my husband," Jill told us. "Jack, this is Miss Brown who rented the pink cottage yesterday and Miss Wilson who is going to take the yellow one, and Mr.—"

"Boyd," he said, and got up to shake hands with the young officer. "If this is the way you treat all your tenants, I'm moving in, too."

"Good," Mason laughed. "Glad to have you."

In spite of Jill's protests I insisted on mopping up the coffee I had spilled. "At least I didn't break the cup."

"You couldn't. It's unbreakable."

"That's the only kind that lasts in this house," the policeman said cheerfully. "It was just crash-bang until we found this stuff. I'm the original bull in the china shop."

"Anyhow," Jill declared, "she could break every dish in this place if she wanted to. She saved Johnny from running right into the open oven door and she got badly burned doing it."

"It's not bad at all," I insisted.

"I keep warning my wife not to leave the oven door open," Mason said. "I fell over it myself the other evening and scraped my shinbone. I've still got a scar."

Jill laughed at him. "You try to sound as though you had been maimed for life."

"How else does a guy get any sympathy around here?"

Her laughter faded. "Jack, honestly you don't know how marvelous Miss Brown was. If she hadn't been so quick—why, she practically slid right across the room—Johnny would have been hurt." She explained to me, "He's just learning to walk and he tries anything, but he's not steady on his feet. I don't dare think what will happen when he discovers the swimming pool."

Jack Mason was young and good-looking and as friendly as his wife. "We're mighty grateful to you, Miss Brown. Hadn't you better see a doctor about that burn?"

"Certainly not," I assured him. I had made the worst possible mistake by doing something that attracted attention to me. And yet no one could sit by and not protect a baby. "It's nothing at all."

"Well, if you are sure." He looked dubious. "Hey, how about some lunch, Jill, for a hard-working man?"

"Right away, but I want to show Mr. Boyd the green cottage first."

"I'll show him the place while you get some lunch."

I thanked Jill for her hospitality and touched the baby's silky cheek with a finger. Somewhat to my surprise Marilyn strolled with me to the door of my cottage. If she expected me to imitate Jill's indiscriminate hospitality and ask her in, she was mistaken.

"I'll be seeing you around," she said. "Sure startled you when that policeman appeared, didn't it? Anyone would have thought you expected to be arrested." She gave me a measuring look. "At least we've got two attractive guys here. Boyd is real distinguished and, my dear, did you get a load of that cop's face? Best-looking thing I've seen in a long, long time. I warn you, I'm going to give you a run for your money where he is concerned."

"I'm not in the running. Anyhow, he is married. He has a nice wife and she has been very nice to us."

"Well, that's her lookout. And I got the idea you have the edge with Boyd. He sure fell for you. Couldn't take his eyes off you. Just my luck to run into competition." She shrugged and turned away, walking with an exaggerated movement of the hips.

Before Jack Mason and Mr. Boyd reached my cottage, I had closed the door and I sagged against it, feeling drained and limp. The sudden appearance of the man with the white Pontiac coupled with the sight of the policeman standing in the doorway had shaken me.

There had been a moment when I had expected, as Marilyn had seen, the policeman would put me under arrest or at least take me in for questioning. But if anyone had to notice that sheer terror I had experienced when I caught sight of Jack Mason, I was relieved that it was Marilyn Wilson and not the man Boyd. But what wretched luck! This was the first place I had really liked and I had settled under the very eyes of the police. For the first time in my life I wished that I knew something about police procedure. Were all policemen briefed about missing persons? How much was known about Will and me and how serious was my position from the standpoint of the law? Would my present address afford protection from Fitz or would it put me in danger of being recognized by the police? But what made me feel cold with dismay was the knowledge that Boyd knew who I was and he must be following me, though I couldn't figure out what he wanted of me. Was he Fitz's deputy? If so, was it the stolen money he was after or had he come to carry out Fitz's threat?

Anyhow, the combination of Boyd and the policeman settled the matter for me. Even the fact that Will was near at hand and that I had seen him just the day before carried no weight now. I wrote out an advertisement, dressed for the street, and went out to get in the Volkswagen. I was not surprised to see the white Pontiac parked at the curb as I drove off.

I suppose newspapers are accustomed to odd advertisements. In any case, the girl who took mine counted the words and told me how much it would be, but she didn't even look up. It appeared next morning among the PERSONALS:

KILROY must end intolerable situation at once or will surrender hatbox without delay. Scarlet

Kilroy and Scarlet were the code names Will had decided on in case we had to get in touch with each other, but we were not, he had warned me, to advertise except in a real emergency.

Now all I could do was to wait. Marilyn Wilson had moved in the afternoon before, bringing with her, I saw in dismay, a guitar. The Boyd man took possession of his cottage that morning. He traveled light, with only one suitcase and some suits on hangers slung over his shoulder. Later he went out and returned with a couple of brown-paper bags of groceries.

Marilyn was lying beside the pool, wearing a bikini, a transistor radio blasting out rock and roll. She waved to him. "Hi there, neighbor!"

"Good morning, Miss Wilson. Nice to be able to do some sun-bathing in February, isn't it?"

She shut off the radio with its persistent and maddening beat. "So you aren't a native Californian."

"New England, but I can't live there any more. The doctors tell me I need a warm climate." He did not have a New England accent, though his voice and manner of speaking were familiar in a way.

"Worse things can happen than being ordered to live in a warm climate."

"You're telling me," he said feelingly.

Marilyn patted the chair next to hers. "Sit down and get acquainted."

"I'd like to, but right now I must put away this food and get off some letters. But later, I hope."

"So you are going to do your own cooking."

"This is mostly canned stuff and frozen dinners. Maybe later on I'll branch out and be more ambitious."

"Popovers?"

He laughed. "It's unlikely."

"How about having dinner with me tonight? Popovers and an old-fashioned pot roast with potatoes and carrots and onions cooked in the gravy?"

"Lady, you've made a sale provided you let me supply the cocktails."

"Swell. About seven?"

"What do you drink?"

"Martinis."

"I knew we were kindred spirits." Boyd put down one of his brown-paper bags while he unlocked the door of the green cottage.

I cursed myself for a fool. In a moment of panic I had put that advertisement in the paper and Will was bound to answer it. The chances were that he would leave a letter under my door sometime in the night, as he had done before. And if he did come, he would be walking into a trap. Belatedly I was aware that if Boyd was working for Fitz, which was the only reason I could imagine for his following me, I too would be in real danger.

Sometime in the early afternoon I eased open the door. Marilyn had set out a few minutes earlier, probably to get in supplies for her dinner. From Boyd's cottage there came the tap of a typewriter. I slipped out as noiselessly as I could. The white Pontiac was at the curb when I drove off. After a few blocks I made a U turn and came back. When I passed the apartment building, the Pontiac was still there and I drew a long breath of relief. At least the man was not following me now.

I drove for hours, with no destination in view, just with a desire to feel free. As well as I could, I tried to thrust out of my mind the danger in which I might have put Will by my impulsive action in advertising. There was nothing I could do now to rectify my mistake. Anyhow, Will had a capacity for landing on his feet; certainly he had been more successful than I at remaining undetected. People had recognized me a score of times but, to the best of my knowledge, no one had recognized Will. And yet, with that flaming red hair and his loud sports jacket and those odd frames on the dark glasses he should have been easy to spot. That he still had the glasses and the jacket I knew, because he had been wearing them each time I saw him.

Where he was and how he had managed to conceal himself so completely I could not imagine. Small wonder that people who had not seen him, as I had, believed that he was dead. Not many people are able to vanish without a single trace. A living person must have food and a place to sleep, and he must be able to venture into the streets, at least occasionally. No one can remain hidden forever. But though I racked my brains, I could not figure out where Will had found sanctuary.

The sun was hot and the air cool. As usual, when I had the choice, I drove toward the mountains, through avenues that were palm-lined, seeing bright green grass, gaily colored houses, more gaily colored flowers.

Driving rests me, keeps my hands occupied, and leaves my mind free. I must have driven like this for hundreds of miles, at one time and another, working out various problems. As usual, I did not attempt to direct my thoughts, just left the problem to my subconscious and, again as usual, it worked. True, I could not prevent Will from coming to the pink cottage to leave me a letter, but I could wait for him, even if I waited all night, and I could warn him of the danger posed by Boyd. And I could see him and talk to him and touch him.

Once I was aroused out of my absorption in my problems by awareness of a familiar road. I saw the beautifully trimmed hedge that sheltered the house and grounds from curious eyes, and realized that I had driven to the Hepburn place. Automatically I braked and let the car slide to a stop outside the open iron gates. I was almost unbearably tempted to go in.

I wanted to tell Mrs. Hepburn the whole story and ask her husband to help Will and me find a way out of the ugly mess.

I didn't go in, of course. I had, of my own free will, helped to shield a thief and a murderer. I had acted in defiance of every principle I had. And without excuse, except my love for Will. Fond as they were of me, the Hepburns would not condone my action. I was outside the law and by my own fault. I have never felt as lonely as I did in that hour.

Will. Tonight he would come to leave me a letter in answer to my frantic advertisement. And this time I was going to see him and implore him to take me with him, wherever he went. At night the patio was dark and the pool unlighted because after the sun went down it was too chilly for swimming. I should be able to keep my vigil unseen. I stopped at a drive-in and got a chicken sandwich which I could eat in the patio and not risk missing Will by cooking a dinner.

When I got back, the Pontiac was still at the curb. As usual the door marked MANAGER was open and Jill hailed me as I went by. "Hi, there! How's the burn? Hadn't I better put more stuff on it?"

It was a heavenly relief to feel the cool ointment on my arm, which she applied with a moan of distress when she saw how deep the burn was.

"It must have kept you awake all night."

"Of course not. It looks a lot worse than it feels," I lied. "How's the son and heir?"

"Completely maddening. I'm thinking of giving him back to the Indians."

"Don't you dare!"

There were lights in Boyd's cottage. The draperies were wide open and I could see him still at the typewriter. There was a gleam of light from behind the draperies at Marilyn's, but there was no sign of her. Probably, I thought, she was busy in her kitchen, pursuing her simple-minded objective of finding the way to a man's heart.

In front of my door there was an advertising circular and I bent automatically to pick it up, not because I was interested in it but because I dislike clutter.

As I put the key in the lock, the door swung open. For one delirious moment all I could think was that Will had come. Even the danger did not seem to matter. I crossed the living room in a flash and then stood at the bedroom door, staring. Marilyn Wilson was calmly going through my clothes closet.

"Well!" I gasped.

She turned around, as cool as though she had every right to be there. "I'm in the midst of getting dinner and I haven't any flour. I've looked everywhere. I hope you don't mind."

For sheer effrontery that took the prize. "I rarely keep flour in my bedroom."

"I guess when you are desperate, you look anywhere." She nodded as I stepped back to let her pass me on the way out.

"How did you get in?"

"The key to my cottage happens to fit yours."

"I'll ask for a new lock tomorrow."

"That might be a good idea," she agreed, "and you can report me to our attractive cop, of course." She met my eyes, smiled, and strolled back to her own cottage, still perfectly self-possessed. I knew then that she felt secure; she was aware that I wouldn't dare report the searching of my cottage to the police.

So there were two people, Boyd and Marilyn, both of whom knew my identity and who had rented cottages the day after I moved in. I wondered why I had not guessed at once that they were working together. Marilyn's dinner invitation had been much too prompt.

This time it seemed that Fitz really had me fenced in.

SIX

It was by the sheerest chance that I found Will's letter. I had tossed the advertising circular on the bed while I removed my wig. The letter had been tucked inside and it had fallen on the carpet. When I picked it up and saw the familiar printing on the envelope, I was so sick with disappointment at first in having missed him again that I did not even open it.

Then I reminded myself that somehow he had managed to come to the cottage and get away undetected under the very eyes of my two inquisitive and suspicious neighbors. I couldn't imagine how he had accomplished it until I remembered noticing vaguely that circulars had been left outside all the cottages, the vacant as well as the rented. No one would pay attention to people delivering advertising circulars. They are practically invisible.

"Darling," I read in Will's painstaking printing, "I saw your ad this morning. You'll be as happy as I am to know that Fitz has seen the light. I went to his apartment yesterday and had a painful meeting with him. He's found a safe way to get out of the country and was only waiting until he could see me. He feels like hell about the whole thing. He said he had tried to reach me but he didn't know how to find me. He swore he wouldn't harm you. Of course he's in a sweat about the money. He doesn't want it now, but he's afraid of it. There's still a murder rap waiting for him. We talked it over and he agreed that I was to turn it in anonymously to the police. So leave the hatbox in a locker at the terminal where we checked our stuff while we hunted for an apartment when we were first married. Put the key in a plastic bag and fasten it under the fourth plank of that little Japanese bridge at the entrance to your building. I'll take over. Then send yourself a telegram and leave in the morning, driving to Las Vegas. I'll make a reservation in the name of Helen Brown at the Big Dollar Motel where I will join you in a few days. Perhaps all this caution isn't necessary, but I want to be sure you are safe when the news breaks about the money being returned, just in case— Anyhow, it's nearly over now and you are my dearest love. Will."

I sat staring at the letter for a long time before I realized what had happened to me. I was afraid to tell Will the truth about the hatbox. He was going to be terribly angry because I had not followed his instructions. My breaking point, however, was that he did not intend to see me tonight. I was just to move on again. This time to Las Vegas.

The extent of my rebellion startled me. I had carried out my part of the bargain. The separation that was to have lasted a few days or a few weeks at most had gone on for six months in which time I had become a woman wanted by the police. But this time I refused to go on, to spend any more time in hiding. I had to see Will face to face before I moved one more step.

"I found your letter," I wrote at last, "but I meant it about this intolerable situation. We've got to meet and talk. Now. I won't agree to put it off any longer, even if I'm not safe from Fitz. I'm sick of having people believe that I am a murderer and hiding out somewhere with a lover. It's queer, isn't it, that Fitz, who always hated me, is suspected of being my lover.

"Please, Will, please let's end this now. I don't have the hatbox with me so I can't follow your instructions right away. It's in the only safe place I could think of. Tonight I'll be waiting for you, love. All night if necessary. Don't slip away before we have talked. I can't take much more. Don't fail me. Helen."

In the kitchen I got a little plastic bag, one of those that comes in a big roll and you tear them off, one at a time. I put my letter in it and, to weigh it down so it wouldn't float on the water I dropped in the key that I had used to open a canned ham. Then I fastened the bag with one of the ties that come with them and switched out my light before opening the door.

This time there were no lights in Boyd's cottage but Marilyn's was lighted up like a birthday cake and the draperies were wide open. I wondered whether that had not been Boyd's idea. He had struck me as a wary bird who could take care of himself.

I went quietly through the patio and under the archway to the dramatic entrance to the main building with its Polynesian trappings, its palms, and its running water. I knelt down on the wooden bridge and tied the plastic bag under the fourth plank, starting nervously when a goldfish darted over my fingers. Then I nearly fell in when I heard a voice say, "You fishing for your dinner, Miss Brown?"

I looked up at the tall good-looking boy in a T-shirt and shorts who laughed down at me. "I was afraid I had lost an earring but luckily it fell on the bridge and not in the water."

He reached down a hand to help me up. I couldn't refuse it without being ungracious, but I thanked him stiffly as I got to my feet.

"How's the burn?" he asked. "Jill and I are mighty grateful to you. The kid could have been badly hurt; he's just a toddler and so far he falls a lot better than he walks, unless someone holds his hand."

In relief I realized that this pleasant young man was Jack Mason, the policeman, and not a stranger trying to make a pick-up. In spite of his casual tone I could see that he was bursting with pride in his small and comely son.

"He's a dear little boy," I said, and hovered until he had gone into his apartment and shut the door. Then

I settled myself in a chair that had a clear view through the archway and onto the bridge. Now that the sun had gone down the air was chilly and I regretted not having equipped myself with a sweater or a light coat, but I did not dare risk leaving my vantage point. Will was bound to come to collect the locker key because lock boxes are opened every twenty-four hours, and he would prefer to get the hatbox at night rather than during the day when the terminal was crowded. And this time I did not intend to miss him. This time there was going to be a showdown.

I ate my sandwich, wished I had another, and sat hugging my arms in an effort to keep warm, though the burned place on my arm hurt horribly when it rubbed against my dress. I had barely settled down for my vigil when Marilyn's door opened and she came out, followed by Boyd. Apparently the dinner had been a success, for they both seemed to be in high spirits. All the same, I suspected that it was Boyd's idea that they leave the cottage.

They sat at the far end of the pool and, as Jack had switched off the patio lights, leaving nothing but a single light at the entrance, I did not think they could possibly see me. The light was an imitation paper lantern, more decorative than useful, but at least it shed enough illumination to prevent anyone from falling into the pool.

Marilyn had brought out her guitar and she made the night hideous with songs that compensated for a lack of melody by the incessant and tireless beat of the tide on the shore. Fortunately she had a low-pitched voice without shrillness or stridency, but even so I found the music maddening.

As it got late, I began to wish anxiously that they would go. They must not be here when Will arrived. If he had been alarmed by my living in a policeman's house, what would he think if he knew that I was hedged in by people who knew my identity?

After what seemed to be hours, Boyd said good

night and thanked Marilyn for a wonderful dinner and a pleasant evening. They were standing at the open door of her cottage and I saw her lift her face for his kiss, in what seemed to be an accustomed gesture, before going inside.

I stirred restlessly, my eyes aching from their strained search of the dim archway for a familiar figure. Then I caught my breath as a shoe scraped on the cement beside the pool and a chair creaked with a man's weight.

"You seem to enjoy rock and roll, Miss Brown." That was Boyd's pleasant voice with something hauntingly familiar about it.

"It's got something."

I could hear the amusement in his voice. "It certainly has." He turned a pocket flashlight on his watch. "Only ten," he said in surprise. "I thought it would be much later."

"You aren't very complimentary to your hostess."

He stretched out his legs as though he was settling down indefinitely and I didn't know how to get rid of him. Somehow I had to be alone when Will came. *Go away*, I told him mentally. *Go away*. With all my strength I willed him to leave me, but it didn't work.

"Aren't you chilly?" he asked.

"A bit, but I couldn't sleep. I thought it might help if I came out here where it's cool and quiet."

"Quiet," he said reflectively, and I remembered the rock and roll. Damn the man.

So we sat and I waited. But no one came.

"It's odd, you know, our being here together," he said at last, breaking a long uneasy silence. "Two New Englanders seeking sunnier skies."

"I've never heard an accent like yours in New England, Mr. Boyd," I said, carrying the war into enemy territory.

He was amused rather than embarrassed. "I seem to have slipped up there. Don't you find that drifting around makes for rather a lonely life?" Apparently this was a game he could play better than I.

"Drifting?"

"Let's see, this is your eighth move in six months, isn't it?"

So there was no possible doubt left. Boyd knew not only my identity but he was familiar with my movements for the past six months.

"I like it."

"I'd have said you were the kind of woman who wants roots. Anyone seeing you with the little Mason boy would think you would like one of your own. You leaped like a gazelle when he stumbled toward that hot oven door. Good reflexes."

I didn't intend to have the talk be about myself. "Have you any children of your own?"

"I'm not married. Probably I wouldn't make a good job of it. I don't seem to understand kids. I don't speak their language: the ones who go off the beam, the hippies, the junkies, the ones who have deliberately cut off all normal restraints. I don't understand what makes them tick."

"But a lot of that," I pointed out, "is a protest against their environment. Every generation has done it in one way or another."

"Sure, people have always protested," he said impatiently. "What burns me is that these kids get hooked on a way of life which will destroy them in the long run. I don't say they are entirely to blame. The people who get them started on dope, the ones who mislead them—they are the real criminals, though I must say that kids from sixteen to twenty ought to be capable of some independent judgment. Or maybe I'm too hard, too unsympathetic. I'm damned if I know."

"I suppose," I commented, laughing, "you accepted all the shibboleths of your group without argument or protest."

"A palpable hit! Sure I protested. But I didn't stone the police or desecrate the flag or try to undermine the whole system."

"It's a good system on the whole."

"Oh, I agree. But without respect for law and order, how long can it last?"

"It strikes me as having a fairly firm foundation," I said mildly. "Harsh words, as my old nurse used to say, break no bones."

"How far would you be willing to go to uphold law and order if your own personal well-being was at stake?"

So all the preliminary skirmishing had simply been getting him in position to strike.

"I suppose we all hope we'd stand firm, but we can't know our own caliber until we are tested. I suppose it's a bit like a man going into battle or a burning house or up against an armed man. You hope you'll behave well and you are afraid you won't."

"What would you regard as a real test?"

"What do you think should be done to meet the kind of situations we have now?" I countered.

I half expected him to be evasive, but he answered promptly, as though he had given it a lot of thought. "I'd like to publish all the facts, to make it impossible for people to go on believing in the Emperor's New Clothes. I'd like to track down the people who corrupt and mislead, and take them out of circulation forever."

"That sounds rather ruthless."

"How else do you fight the destroyers?" This was a rhetorical question and he did not wait for a reply. "Not by burying your head in the sand. Not," he hesitated, seeking a word, failing to find it, "not by running away."

There it was again, but I wasn't sure whether I was his target or someone or something else. "Then what are you really doing to help matters, Mr. Boyd? Are you starting your own private crusade or joining someone else's?"

"It's a private crusade. At least, it started that way. But a private crusade tends to ramify. Perhaps we can't become deeply involved unless there is a personal issue at stake. When something unspeakable happens to you, you can't remain detached."

"Was it really that bad?"

"It wasn't good. Not good at all. I had a kid brother, a nice guy, an A student. Like most intelligent kids, he was curious. He wanted to try things for himself instead of taking someone's word for them. Or perhaps that wasn't so intelligent. Anyhow, he was offered some marijuana cigarettes and he experimented with them. Then he was given heroin and after using it only a couple of times he got hooked."

A car slowed down outside and I was alert, holding my breath. Then it went on and I relaxed. Intent on his own thoughts, Boyd did not seem to notice.

"He didn't tell me about it," he said heavily. "I don't know whether he thought I wouldn't understand or whether he was ashamed. Or both, of course. And I was out of the country at the time. Sometimes it is hard to put things down in black and white when you could talk them out easily, face to face. I think he tried to handle it for himself, but he got in too deep. He needed more and more of the stuff, so his helpful friend showed him how to get the money by stealing it. Well, he hijacked a payroll delivery and he was picked up. He was terribly young, only sixteen. I flew back home, got him out on bail, and intended to put him in the hands of a doctor, but by the time I went back with the doctor, Ben was dead."

I had been listening with only half my attention because I was waiting for Will. But when Boyd mentioned the payroll robbery I was alert and the end of his story jolted me badly, though he had been speaking rather flatly, as though deliberately holding a lid down on his emotions.

"How awful! You mean he killed himself?"

"That's what the doctor and the police assumed. He was—hanging when we found him. But I believed then and I believe now that he was murdered to prevent him from telling anyone the name of the man who had used him to stage the robbery, who had got away with the money and left Ben to take the punishment. That's my job right now. I'm looking for a man. I intend to find him."

I guessed now what Boyd was after. He was looking for Harry Fitzhugh and he believed I could lead him to his quarry. All those comments about the law and respect for the law had been to find out just how corrupt I was, how far I would go to protect Harry Fitzhugh. Of all possible situations this is the last I would have dreamed of.

I think I would have confided in him then and there, assuming that we were allies rather than enemies, if he had not given a stifled exclamation and leaped toward the bridge, catching hold of a thin, almost gaunt, boy who had fished up the little plastic bag. He had come so quietly that I had been unaware of his approach.

The boy turned like a startled wild animal, jerked away, and lashed out, kicking Boyd, who doubled up with agony. By the time he had picked himself up painfully, the boy had disappeared. Boyd came back slowly, the plastic bag dangling from his fingers.

"Yours, I think."

"Why?"

"I saw you put it there, Mrs. Gates."

SEVEN

Boyd said, "You are Mrs. Gates, aren't you?"

"You ought to know who I am, Mr. Boyd. You've been following me for a long time, haven't you?"

"Yes, I've been following you." There was nothing threatening in his voice. Indeed, he sounded almost friendly.

"I suppose I should be flattered at arousing so much interest, but isn't it duplication of effort for two of you to be checking on me at the same time?"

"Two?" I would have sworn that he was genuinely astonished.

"This afternoon I found Marilyn Wilson searching my cottage. She told me it just happened that her key fitted my door. When I found her, she was going through the clothes closet and she explained that she was looking for flour, presumably for the popovers which are the way to a man's heart."

"Presumably," he agreed, and there was laughter in his voice. Then he sobered. "What made you believe that she and I are working together?"

"You arrived at the same time. You both know who I am. There can't be two people who would go to such lengths to have me followed. Did he send you and Marilyn Wilson to find out where the money is or to kill me so Will will have to come forward?"

"Who in the name of God are you talking about?"

"I'm talking about a man named Harry Fitzhugh. You've heard his name, haven't you?"

"Yes," Boyd said, "but you are quite wrong. Incredibly wrong. He didn't send me here, Mrs. Gates."

"Then, if he didn't send you, you are looking for him."

"Yes," he said again.

"I thought that must be it when you were telling me about your young brother. He was involved with Fitz, wasn't he?"

"Yes," Boyd said grimly.

"I'm terribly sorry for you and your brother, but you are wasting your time with me if you expect me to lead you to Harry Fitzhugh. I haven't seen him in more than six months and I hope to God I never see him again! He's done nothing but harm. You know yourself what he did to your brother and that's only part of it. He hijacked a payroll—that seems to be a specialty of his—and killed a guard. He told my husband that he had to have the money to pay for an operation that would save his father's life, but the money turned out to be in marked bills.

"Will has always been devoted to Fitz. He never had any brothers and he felt as responsible for Fitz as though he were his kid brother. He did his best to persuade him to return the money and explained that he could not spend it because as soon as any of it turned up he would be facing not only a robbery charge but a murder charge. But Fitz wouldn't listen. He said if Will gave back the money, he would kill me. And Will—you don't know what he is—tried to protect me and at the same time save Fitz from himself."

Boyd listened, with strained attention, while I told him how Will had made me go into hiding from Fitz and then tried to lead him away from me. All these months of sacrifice for Fitz, a thief and a murderer. My clenched fists beat on my knees in anger. "But Fitz wouldn't give up. He took that snapshot of me that appeared on television and in the papers. He must have given it to them to smoke me out. He'll never rest until he either gets the money or punishes Will by killing me. Right now Will is trying to believe that Fitz has changed, but he can't be sure."

"Then your husband has seen this man Fitz."

I nodded and realized that Boyd could not see me in the darkness. "Yes, he's seen him and talked to him."

"Then, Mrs. Gates, I'm going to stick to you like a burr. Because you are going to lead me to your husband and he is going to lead me to Fitz."

"Will doesn't sell out his friends."

"Where on earth has he managed to hide so successfully, Mrs. Gates? A successful salesman, a man who makes a lot of friends, how the hell can he disappear in so small a community?"

"He is somewhere near. That's all I know. I suppose he didn't think it would be safe for me to know where he is living."

"Do you really expect me to believe that?" He sounded bored. "Oh, come now, Mrs. Gates."

The mockery and incredulity in his voice humiliated me. "I'm telling you the truth. You've got to believe me, unless you are one of the people who think I killed Will, with the help of Fitz."

He laughed softly. "Not at any time. Though the stage setting, from what I read in the papers, put you in a hell of a spot. If I ever saw a prettier set-up for a murder charge, I can't remember it. Everything was there except the corpse, but I suppose that was difficult to arrange. So you've never seen your husband since he went off into the blue."

I could hear the disbelief in his voice. "I've seen him three times. Twice at a distance, waving to me. Once he took my hand and whispered to me in a supermarket. But he was gone before I could speak to him."

Boyd pounced on this, questioning me like a cross-examiner in court. "Actually," he said at last, "you've seen your husband's sports jacket and some unusual sun glasses he used to wear. But you could hardly swear on oath that you saw him, could you?"

"But I—of course I've seen him."

"Suppose you should be picked up for your husband's murder. Could you provide any tangible proof that you have actually seen him since you left your apartment six months ago? Have you any real proof that he is alive?"

"Well, I—oh, of course, I have his letters."

"Can you prove that he wrote them? Could you produce other samples of his writing that would settle the matter beyond doubt?"

"He always prints. He—Mr. Boyd, are you trying to frighten me? Do you believe my husband is dead and someone has been impersonating him, playing a monstrous trick on me?"

"I don't know. I hope with all my heart that he is alive and well." Boyd dangled the little plastic bag. "What was the deal about this?"

I told him that I had been so upset by his arrival as well as the discovery that I lived in a policeman's house that I had put an ad in the paper in which I issued an ultimatum. I wanted to end the situation and I intended to restore the money without any further delay. Then, to my bitter disappointment, Will had left a message while I was out that afternoon, telling me what he wanted done with the hatbox and instructing me to move out at once. He was going to return the money to its owners. I was to leave the hatbox in a locker and put the key in the little bag. But I had decided that this time I would wait for him to come if it took all night. I wanted him to take me away with him, risk or no risk.

Boyd held up the little plastic bag and prodded it. "So the money has been in your custody all the time," he said queerly. "Of all possibilities that is the last one I would have considered. Your husband must trust you."

"Why on earth shouldn't he? You can't believe that either of us wants that money, Mr. Boyd! You can't. Not possibly."

"Some such idea did cross my mind," he admitted.
"But I've been explaining that Will took it only to rotect Fitz and I went along because that's what Vill asked of me."

"You didn't object to having stolen money in your possession? Money with blood on it?"

"Of course I objected! I think it should have gone straight back to the company, even if Fitz was arrested then and there, or even if he tried to kill me. But Will said we couldn't take the chance."

"A very thin story. I'd like to hear just how much credibility it would carry with the police. You have great faith in your husband, Mrs. Gates."

Some mocking overtone in his voice made me say angrily, "Complete faith. Don't doubt that for a moment. From the day we first met. And that was typical of Will and his unselfish goodness." I described how he had come to the welfare agency to give a teen-ager a second chance and help him build a useful life.

It was late and the chill in the air was intensified by a brisk wind. I found myself shivering.

"You are cold," Boyd said. "You ought to go in. He won't be coming tonight."

"I know," I said dully. "You've spoiled everything. And I wanted so terribly to have him come."

"But it wasn't your husband who came," Boyd pointed out. "He sent someone else."

"And now, because you took that bag with my letter, I have no way of reaching him. Haven't you done enough harm? I'll tell you this, Mr. Boyd; you'll never find Fitz by watching me. I suggest you keep an eye on Marilyn Wilson. I think she is working for him."

"Why?"

"Why else would she be spying on me, searching my cottage? Only Fitz would want to know what I was doing or planning."

"You dislike this man Fitzhugh, don't you, Mrs. Gates?"

"No more than he dislikes me; my feeling isn't a patch on his. I saw that the first time I met him."

"Why do you suppose he disliked you at sight?"

"He has immense influence over my husband. I suppose he was afraid I might undermine it." I couldn't keep the bitterness out of my voice. "He needn't have worried about that. Anyhow, I have every reason for hating him. He's a thief and a murderer. You should have seen the face of that dead guard's widow; it would have broken your heart. And look at what he's done to Will and me. It's a terrible position I'm in."

"It's all of that. In fact, I think you still have not grasped clearly just what your position is, Mrs. Gates."

"You mean that television program that said, 'This Woman Wanted'?"

"I think you two are the victims of as sweet a frame-up as I've ever encountered."

"I don't understand."

"That's fairly obvious." He seemed to recall the little plastic bag he had been holding. "Do you mind?"

I shrugged. Now that I had lost my opportunity to get in touch with Will, I didn't seem to mind anything. Boyd took my silence for consent and opened the bag. He pulled out my note, which he read with the help of his pocket flashlight. Then he picked up the key that had fallen on the cement. "What's this?"

"It's a key to open a canned ham. I just wanted something to weigh down the bag."

"Mrs. Gates, I haven't wanted to alarm you, but it is high time you realize that you are in real danger. The boy who came to collect that key must have believed it was in the bag I took away from him. You have simply got to dispose of that hatbox and the money at once. You should do it without an hour's delay."

"If you hadn't stopped that boy, Will would have come by now, knowing that I would be waiting. Everything would be settled, if it hadn't been for you."

"Nothing can be settled until you turn over that money."

So at last he had come to it. That was Boyd's goal. Not me. Not Fitz. The money.

"What have you done with it, Mrs. Gates?"

I was so cold now that my teeth were chattering. "I won't tell you."

"You really are a fool, you know," he said in a tone of cool detachment. "The idiotic stories you fall for. That pitiful tale of Fitzhugh needing money to save his father's life. I've made a considerable study of Fitzhugh and I know that his father died some months ago."

"I didn't fall for that story. Will did. He's a pushover for hard-luck stories and he goes out of his way to help people, as he did Fred."

"Who is Fred?"

"The boy at the welfare agency I told you about, the one Will helped to get a second start in life." I got up, trying to clench my jaws and check the chattering of my teeth.

"Just a minute, Mrs. Gates."

"I'm cold. Terribly cold. Good night, Mr. Boyd." As he laid a restraining hand on my arm I shook it off, went back to my cottage, undressed, and crawled into bed, the blankets high around my shoulders, shaking and shaking. Then I was out of bed in a flash and I ran to jam a chair under the doorknob. I had just remembered that Marilyn's key fitted my lock. It was even possible that Boyd's did, too.

I lay listening to the muted sounds of traffic, the rumble of trucks, the roar of a plane overhead, and the chattering of my teeth. Little by little, the rigidity of my jaw relaxed, the shivering stopped, and I was warm again. The burn on my arm felt like fire, but I had forgotten to get any ointment for it. I'd have to endure the pain until morning. I went over the shocks of the day: the discovery of Marilyn searching my cottage and learning that she knew my identity; the stealthy appearance of the boy who had come to get the key and the sudden viciousness of his attack on Boyd; my bitter awareness that once more the link between Will and me had been snapped. I had built so much on talking to him that I was sick with disappointment.

I tried to analyze Boyd's story, but I didn't know how much I could believe. I had accepted without question his account of his young brother's involvement with Fitz, his growing dependence on drugs, the payroll theft, and the sudden violence that had ended his life.

But what else could I believe? The victim of a frame-up, he had called me. He had planted the idea that Will was dead, that all I could actually identify would be the glasses and the jacket; that even his letters were the work of someone else. Will dead! The terrible thing was that, once the idea was suggested, I couldn't dismiss it. That would account for the long, long delay better than anything else. I wished to heaven I had never seen Boyd. I felt that when he had snatched the plastic bag from Will's messenger he had broken permanently my link to my husband, that something irreparable had happened.

My bedside clock with its radium dial showed half-past two when I heard a light tap at the door. My heart lurched and slowed again. Will had come to me, after all. I pulled on the emerald velvet robe he had given me for my birthday and took time to brush my hair back smoothly and slip a green silk ribbon over it. After all, it had been six months and I wanted him to see me at my best. Then I ran to pull the chair away from the door and open it. Belatedly I remembered to ask, "Who is it?" though I had no doubt at all. I couldn't be this happy for nothing.

"Boyd." His voice was just above a whisper. Before I could move, he had a foot inside. He pushed his way past me and closed the door quietly behind him. Oddly enough, I was not in the least frightened. Knowing that the draperies were drawn, I switched on the light and saw his expression. The robe was one of the most becoming things I had ever owned and it molded my body to the waist, where it fitted snugly, while the full skirt fell to my feet in shimmering folds.

At length he said, "I understand now why Fitzhugh objected to your marriage to another man. He must have been bowled over. A man doesn't see beauty like yours many times in a lifetime."

I was so surprised I could think of no comment to make. Finally I said, "What do you want? It's terribly late."

"I know." He glanced at the chair I had moved away from the door. "That's a good idea. I'll get you a new lock tomorrow."

"Thank you." I waited for him to go.

"There's just one question. What's the name of that boy?" Seeing that I was at a loss, he explained, "The boy on welfare whom your husband helped."

"Oh, you mean Fred?"

"I suppose so. If you handled the case, you must know his last name." Boyd spoke casually, too casually, and I was on guard at once.

"I don't remember. I had a heavy case load." My tone was as casual as his.

Boyd's eyes had moved from my face to my body in that revealing robe. Now they rested on my telltale clenched fists. "What happened to him, do you know?"

I shook my head but I had realized the truth in a flash. The gaunt boy who had come for the key to the lock box was Fred Cook and he must still be in close touch with Will. Now I knew where Will was and why he had been able to remain unseen and undetected for so many months; how he had been able to keep track of my movements without being observed, and to procure food and lodging without being noticed.

Tomorrow I would call the welfare agency trusting that no one there remembered my voice, and ask for the address of a former welfare client, Fred Cook.

EIGHT

As it turned out, I never called the welfare agency to inquire about Fred Cook. That night I lay awake for a long time tormented by Boyd's implication that Will might be dead and that I was the victim of some gigantic hoax. Curiously enough it was his voice when he told me he hoped that Will was alive that alarmed me most. To Boyd, Will was only a signpost leading to Fitz, but to me he was my whole life.

When at last I slept, I had horrible dreams. By morning I was depleted. I didn't know which had been worse, the nightmares or the tormenting thoughts when I was awake.

I slept so late that I fixed a combination breakfast and lunch. It was nearly three when I went to the nearest shopping center to put in some supplies and to a pharmacy where I bought ointment for the burn. For once the big shopping area was nearly empty. In southern California the average housewife waits until almost dinnertime to recall that there is nothing in the house to eat, and then she rushes out to join a mob and do some hasty buying, adding to the already congested traffic.

When I came out of the pharmacy, I saw one of those little three-wheeled electric carts that you find now and then in southern California. They can hold two passengers if neither of them is very big and their average speed seems to be ten to fifteen miles an hour. I had noticed them occasionally and observed that they were usually driven by elderly persons, chiefly women. The driver of the one that had drawn up beside the Volkswagen was no exception. She had white hair that looked as though she never washed it, a gray dress, and a dirty white sweater. She was watching every move I made.

While I put my shopping bag in the back seat of the Volkswagen I pretended not to notice that unswerving stare, but when I started to get into the car she spoke to me. She had a harsh voice, a more vigorous voice than I would have expected of such an old woman.

"Will wants to see you."

The shock moved from my head to my feet and I made myself turn very slowly, my face expressionless. "Are you speaking to me?"

"That's right, Mrs. Gates. Will wanted me to bring you."

"You've made a mistake, I think." I put my key in the switch.

"Wait!" Her voice was louder, more urgent. "There's no mistake unless you make one. Will has been living with Fred and me for the past six months."

A number of the pieces of the puzzle that had bewildered me fell into place. "Then you must be Mrs. Cook, Fred's mother."

She grinned, showing discolored teeth and deep vertical lines like slits in her cheeks. "Well, at least I am Fred's mother."

"I remember that my husband took an interest in Fred and tried to help him."

"We haven't done so bad by Will neither, and don't you forget it. Keeping an eye on you so's he would know when you moved and where you was. Keepin' him out of sight. Fred and me running his errands night and day, and much thanks we get for it." There was enough venom in the old woman's voice to poison her. "It wasn't Fred's fault that he couldn't hang onto that key last night. Some guy jumped him and took it offen him. But Will wouldn't believe him. He nearly beat my Fred to death. Got it in his head that Fred had used the key to take the hatbox for himself. But he never! I know when he's lying. So finally I told Will he could let Fred alone or we'd put him out of the house."

It was a shock to hear this horrible, disreputable woman speak so familiarly of Will. It was even more of a shock to hear her talk of my gentle husband beating a boy almost to death.

"So I told Will to his face we'd had it up to here and he promised to give me a real break when he got the money."

"Just what do you want of me?"

"Will wants that key."

I wouldn't have trusted that old harridan an inch. "I don't have the key." Well, that was true enough.

"Then you had better come along and tell Will yourself. Maybe he'll believe you."

I still didn't trust her. I knew that I might be walking into a trap. But there would be no point in Fred hurting me; and even, at the worst and ugliest, if he tried to force me to tell him where the money was, there was no way he could compel the Hepburns to give it to him. In fact, the Hepburns would not hesitate to have Fred and his mother placed under arrest if they were stupid enough to make threats.

On the other hand, there was a chance that I might find Will and end the nightmare so that we could go back to a normal life with peace and laughter and love in it. So I agreed to leave the Volkswagen and drive with the old woman. I squeezed into the little cart beside her. In spite of my forebodings, I could not keep down the surging hope that I was going to find Will at last.

Some instinct of self-preservation made me watch carefully each time she made a turn in case I should have to find my way back. The section to which she drove me was one I had not seen before. When I went driving I usually headed for the mountains or wide palm-lined avenues with brilliant green lawns and even more brilliant flowers. This was very different. In the short dead-end block there was a filling station, a drive-in—now out of business—that had sold tacos; an empty lot strewn with beer cans, broken bottles, and cardboard containers. And there was the shack, its faded stucco chipped here and there, set on hard-baked earth.

The woman was watching my face. "Yeah," she said. "Not much, is it? Some people have everything. It's not what you deserve that counts in this life. You got to be smart enough to take it."

She preceded me into the shack, which had only four rooms: a living room, bedroom, kitchen, and primitive bath. It was filthy, with curls of gray dust on the floor, a pervasive smell of mice, a couple of dirty glasses on a table and paper plates holding the unappetizing remains of food. I could see all this at a glance and I could see, too, that the place was unoccupied except for Fred's mother and me. Any hope that I would find Will there died at that moment.

I turned fiercely on the old woman, but she wasn't old, not that old, at least. With a sigh of relief she had pulled off her white wig and tossed it on the table so that it fell onto a soiled plate. She had brown hair that had been badly dyed and brown pouches under evil and knowing eyes. She was probably nearer fifty than the seventy-five I had assumed.

"Will isn't here. Why have you brought me to this place?"

Her manner was a curious blend of the hard-boiled and the cringing. "Look here, Mrs. Gates, we've been playing along for six months."

"Where is my husband?"

She ignored my frantic question. "You got to see it our way. Fred ain't so strong. It goes agin him to work regular. It makes him nervous and restless. You can't expect it of him. He's just a kid who's got a right to take it easy. We been keepin' Will under cover. That's a big risk, let me tell you." Her tone shifted suddenly, was threatening. "To cut this short, we know about the money. Will—well, we got him to tell us. He said you have it." She took my arm, digging her bony fingers into the muscle. "Me and Fred deserve a fair cut for all we done. We're going to get it. We got our rights."

"Even if I'd give it to you—and I won't; get that into your head—you couldn't spend it. It's marked money."

"We know that but you don't know much and that's a fact. Sure we can't spend it. But we finally got in touch with a good guy who'll buy it off us. His job is discounting hot money. Maybe he pays us only fifty per cent, but so what? We ain't proud. Then he ships this marked money out of the country where it will be as good as gold. People do it all the time if they have the right connections. We'd have done it at the beginning and not had things draggin' on like this, because we had a good guy lined up, only he died on us and we've had to look for someone else. We never dreamed it would take so long." Her fingers dug deeper into my arm and touched the burn. For a moment the pain made me sick. "So where is it?"

"There's only one thing to be done with that stolen money," I told her. "It has to be returned intact to the people it belongs to."

The concept that anyone could be honest, that anyone could voluntarily relinquish stolen money was too alien for her to grasp. She disbelieved me, but she changed her tactics. Her voice became a whine. "That's not fair. Fred and me deserve a cut. The people it was stolen off of are rich. They don't need it like we do. Lookit this place compared with yours. Why should you have it all? It ain't fair. We got rights."

"Then let Fred work for a living like other men. It won't kill him."

Her hand lashed out, striking me so hard across the face that I staggered backward. "He ain't up to it. Anyhow, that's no business of yours. Tell me where you hid the money or you'll never get out of here."

I was less than half her age and in a lot better physical condition, so I wasn't frightened. Not, at least, for myself. There was only one question that loomed sky-high. "What have you done with Will?"

Like counterpoint came her answer. "What have you done with the money?"

"Listen to me. Even if you could make me tell you where the money is, you couldn't touch it. That is the truth. Unless I were there with you, you couldn't lay hands on a single penny. Not one. The people who are keeping it for me would never surrender it to a stranger. And what's more, you'd be arrested for trying to get it, both you and your precious son."

As she realized that I was telling her the truth, she seemed to wilt and I took instant advantage. I struck off her hand and caught her by her shoulders, forcing her to look at me. "Where is Will? What have you done with him?"

Her eyes wavered, looked almost involuntarily past my shoulder and toward the open bedroom door behind me. I whirled around and then at last I saw him. I ran stumbling across the room, my arms outstretched.

"Will! Oh, love!"

Instead of taking me in his arms, he tried to push me away, but I hung on desperately. His red hair was completely covered by a cap, but I knew that loud checked sports jacket and the odd frames of the dark glasses. Dark glasses in a room as dark as this? I snatched at them and jerked them off.

Just at the moment when I recognized Fred Cook, he slugged me.

II

I don't know how long that blackout lasted. Before I opened my eyes I was aware of my acute discomfort. For one horrified moment, as I tried to move my hands, I thought that I was paralyzed. Then I realized that I had been tied on a chair with my hands behind me.

There were two people in the room, watching me with curiosity but without kindness. One was Fred's mother, her face stamped with all the evil of her life; the other was Fred himself. In the months since I had seen him he had lost so much weight that he was almost emaciated. The pupils of his eyes were mere pinpoints. With a sinking of the heart I realized that he was a dope addict. There was nothing to hope for from Fred. With his terrible need of the drug there would be no use in appealing to him.

I closed my eyes and let my head drop forward on my chest. As long as they believed I was unconscious, they might let me alone. All I could hope for was delay, to play for time. When I moved my head, there was a lancing pain. Fred had struck me unnecessarily hard.

Even while I was pretending to be unconscious, I wondered why I bothered. In a way it would be easier to get the whole thing over as quickly as possible. Now that I knew Will was dead, life did not seem so important. Just the same something in me clung to it, wanted fiercely not to be destroyed.

I wondered dully how those two had managed to kill anyone as agile and strong as Will. Will with his laughter stilled forever. Sickness welled up in my throat. I knew that however desperate Fred might be for money, however unscrupulous his mother, they would never have dared bring me here while Will was alive. I could see what must have happened. Will had trusted Fred and had gone to him for sanctuary. He and his mother had learned of the money Will was carrying, the money I had given him. Knowing Will, it seemed probable to me that he had shown it to them to assure them that he could pay for his food and lodging. Perhaps they had taken it from him. Perhaps they had caught him off guard and tortured him into telling why he was seeking sanctuary. In some way they had learned of the stolen money. All this time those brief appearances at a careful distance and the printed letters had been the work of Fred Cook, keeping me docile until he and his mother could find a safe man to dispose of the marked money for them.

A fist was thrust under my chin and snapped my head back brutally. "Okay," Fred said, "let's give up the fun and games. Who is the guy who took that key off me last night?"

I looked at him as steadily as I could, but I didn't answer him. He slapped me across the face, making me gasp with pain.

"Who is he?" Fred repeated.

I looked at him, at the eyes which betrayed his drug addiction, at the loose mouth with its indications of degeneracy, and saw that he was doomed. But I did not find him pitiful; I found him disgusting. Something of my thought must have appeared in my face. He took a deep drag on the cigarette that wobbled between his lips and pressed the lighted tip into the burn I had got on the oven. I cried out with the pain.

"Who is he?"

I did not answer.

Again he dragged on the cigarette and this time it was pressed against my throat. When I cried out, he gave a high nervous giggle of pleasure.

"Who is he?" The coal of the cigarette glowed red as he brought it down to my face, moving it back and forth so near my eyes that I could feel its heat on my lids. "This time it will be your left eye. Next time—"

Panic almost shut off my voice. Then I screamed, "No! No! Please don't! Please!" There was no pride left, no desire even to keep my faith with Will, no shame of betrayal. Nothing but a quivering jelly of terror.

"Who is he?"

"Boyd! His name is Boyd! He lives in the green cottage. He—"

"Okay. Now we're cooking with gas." As though the

temptation to inflict pain was more than he could withstand, even after my capitulation, he jabbed his cigarette toward my eyes. I jerked my head back and felt the searing pain on the delicate skin of my lower lid, not a sixteenth of an inch below the eye itself. I heard the wild scream that tore from my throat in terror and pain. And, in the quiet that followed, someone banged on the door and shouted. Fred and his mother exchanged some startled words and then Fred picked up a little leather strap, weighted on one end, and swung it, striking me behind the ear.

NINE

When I regained consciousness for the second time, I thought for one hideous moment that I was blind. The burn under my left eye was agonizing. Then I realized that the room was in total darkness. At first I was aware of nothing but my own body. All of me hurt. My arms were sore and my shoulders were cramped and lame. I was still strapped on the chair. The cigarette burns on my arm and throat felt like fire. My head ached horribly.

Then memory came back. Fred Cook and his mother had done this to me and Will was gone. Gone forever. All along it had been Fred, Fred wearing Will's dark glasses and his jacket.

Fred? Dope addict and degenerate. His mother, vicious, unscrupulous, vile. But they were not intelligent. Neither of them was capable of planning this kind of crime. Neither of them could have succeeded in tricking Will. Neither of them could have written the letters that carried the very cadence of Will's voice. That could only be the work of someone who knew him intimately, and that was Will's bad angel Harry Fitzhugh.

Of course, Boyd had seen it from the beginning, and he had tried to make me see it for myself. Will and I had been the victims of a frame-up. All along it was Fitz who had written the scenario, who had taken the precaution of leaving the marked money in my hands until it was safe to dispose of it. He had not foreseen the delay until he could find another man to discount it, but by arranging the stage-setting that had made me appear to have killed Will, he had hoped to make it impossible for me to go to the police.

Tears rolled down my cheeks for Will, for the happiness that would never come again, for all the gaiety that had been snuffed out. And the fear came back. My tears would betray me. Fred would light another cigarette and this time it would be my eyes.

I held my breath, listening, but no one spoke. Nevertheless I felt that I was not alone in the little shack. Or perhaps the faint movements I had heard might be rats in this filthy place. Then someone stirred and cursed and I gasped in sheer horror. My eyes were wide open now, peering through the darkened room.

"Helen?"

"Who are you?"

"Ron. Ronald Boyd. How badly are you hurt?"

"Nothing serious. Where are you?"

"On the floor near the door, trussed up like a chicken," he raged.

"That's my fault. I was to blame for Fred bringing you here and doing this to you. I—when he said he'd burn out my eyes I—I told him you had taken the key. I'm sorry. I'm truly sorry and ashamed. I didn't know I was such a coward. You remember, when we were talking last night, I said you couldn't tell about yourself until you were tested. Well, I know about myself now."

"He burned you?" There was an ugly tone in Ronald's usually pleasant and relaxed voice.

"Not too badly. Anyhow, that's not the important thing. They killed Will."

He gave a muffled exclamation. "Are you sure about that?"

"Oh, yes. There's no doubt at all. Fitz must have planned it from the beginning. All along it has been Fred Cook wearing Will's jacket and his dark glasses and a cap because he doesn't have red hair. But that was what you tried to tell me, wasn't it?"

"Not quite. I was just pointing out that, if you were accused of your husband's murder, you wouldn't have a single scrap of proof that would stand up under examination that he is actually alive."

"The worst is that I don't even know what Fitz— did with him."

"Where do you think Fitz is?"

"I wish I knew. He's been having Fred and his mother watch me to see where I went, because of the money. Now, apparently, he believes it is safe to have it in his own hands. Fred's mother said it could be discounted. Do you understand how that works?"

"Yes."

"That's what they have been waiting for all this time. They had a man whom they knew but he died and it was hard to find someone else. They hadn't counted on that. I suppose they thought it was safest to leave the money with me, but now they want it."

"And you wouldn't give it to them." Again there was that odd note in his voice.

"Not if I rotted!" I was taken aback by my own savagery. The controls with which I had grown up seemed to be slipping badly. "No one is going to profit by the money that caused the guard to die and now has killed my husband. No one!"

"Where are you?"

"In the middle of the room, tied to a chair."

"Both hands and feet?"

"My hands are tied behind my back but my feet are free. I suppose they knew I couldn't go far with that chair lashed on my back."

"Do you think you could possibly hobble out to the kitchen and look for a knife?"

"Not possibly."

He waited for a moment and then said thoughtfully, "Have you considered what would happen if someone set fire to this place? We'd both be roasted alive.

There are easier ways of dying, if that's what you are set on doing."

The picture was vivid before my eyes. "All right, I'll try."

After a few attempts to get on my feet, strapped to the chair so that I had to remain bent practically double, I decided my best bet would be to crawl. At the first attempt I toppled over on my face and the chair crashed down on top of me. The pain in my head was so awful I lay there until some of the first agony had begun to diminish. I could hear Ronald thrashing around madly and futilely, trying to release himself.

"Are you hurt?"

I realized that he had been saying it over and over while I was trying to cope with the pain. To my own surprise I found myself laughing, shrill, hysterical gusts of laughter. Every part of me, except for my numb hands, hurt and he had asked, "Are you hurt?" I thought it was screamingly funny.

"Stop that!" His voice was like a whiplash. "Hold your breath. You can if you try. Now take another deep one and hold it as long as you can. You can't afford to indulge in hysterics."

Indulge. If he wanted to make me angry, he succeeded without half trying.

"Try to pull yourself together, Helen. We've got to get out of this place before they come back."

That was probably the one threat that would have made me ignore the lancing pain in my head and begin to crawl slowly toward the kitchen. I would make a few feet, carrying the chair on my back like a king-size papoose, unable to keep my balance because my hands were tied behind me, and then fall forward on my face, unable to protect it, my cheeks bruised and grazed on that filthy floor, which was made of rough planks. Then I would haul myself up and start again.

Only when I had reached the kitchen—I could feel the linoleum, which had a sour smell but at least had no splinters—did it occur to me that I could not reach the drawers and, even if I could, I could not pick up a knife with my hands tied behind me. I began to cry in sheer frustration.

"What is it?" Ronald shouted.

When I had explained, he began to thrash around again, trying to free himself, but without result.

"And anyhow," I called, "even if I could see, which I can't; even if I could reach for a knife, which I can't, I couldn't cut us free, tied up like this. We'll never get out of here alive." My voice rose. "That's what Fred's mother said. Never get out alive!"

"We've got to get away from here. Okay, so a knife is out. Now what else would work? Helen!" He sounded excited. "I'm the world's most blasted fool. There's a knife in the pocket of my pants; in fact, I'm lying on it right now."

"You might have thought of that before," I said furiously, and backed out of the kitchen and toward the sound of his voice, moving a few feet, falling on my face, moving again. Only when I heard a grunt did I realize that I had misjudged the distance and had rammed him with a chair leg. For hours it seemed to me that we maneuvered around each other in the dark. I was crawling and Ronald was sort of hitching himself along, while we tried to get in position so I could reach his pocket. About all I did was to bombard him with blows from those damned chair legs, and he couldn't even duck.

"It's no good," I said at last, and lay where I had fallen on the floor beside him. "I couldn't use my hands now even if I could reach the knife. There's no circulation."

He must have heard the complete defeat in my voice but he refused to let me give up hope. "All right. Keep your shirt on. It will be all right." I could hear his strained breathing and then I felt him give a sudden, violent jerk and gasp as though trying to cope with a stab of pain.

"What is it?"

"I snapped the cord. Just a minute now while I get

my knife." After a couple of minutes, during which he seemed to be doing a great deal of grunting, I realized he was extricating himself from the cord with which he had been, as he said, trussed up like a chicken. He got cautiously to his feet, as though checking to see that all parts of him were in working order, and then he groped his way to the door, feeling along the wall for a light switch.

"There's only a single drop light and it's in the center of the room," I told him and he came back, stepped heavily on my foot and sprawled over the chair, his weight knocking the breath out of me and convincing me, for at least a minute, that I had been half killed. He scrambled to his feet, cursing, and groped around. Finally a forty-watt unshaded bulb came to life.

Then he was cutting the cord that bound my hands and lifting the chair off my back. My shoulders were so strained from being pulled back that it was agony to move them. He picked me up and gave an exclamation of horror when he saw my face. Later, when I got a look at myself, I could understand it. My face was filthy, swollen and discolored from banging on the floor over and over; there were deep scratches, as though a cat had clawed me, from which the blood seeped, a result of scraping along the unfinished wood. In fact, it was a wonder that one of the splinters had not gouged out an eye. The cigarette burns were red and ugly. Tears had left dirty streaks on my cheeks. The blond wig with its beehive hair-do had been pushed to the back of my head, which ached horribly. There were welts on my wrists where the cord had bitten in. And my bloodless hands were as white as those of the dead.

Compared with me, Ronald was in fairly good shape. He was stiff and lame from being tied up for hours, but he had been struck only once and, though his head must have hurt like mad, he assured me that he was fine. His wrists were swollen and lacerated and bleeding from his struggle to snap the cord that had bound them.

He put me back in the chair and went out to the kitchen where he filled a bowl with warm water. When he came back he knelt beside me, tossed off my silly wig, and took a clean handkerchief out of his jacket pocket with which he bathed my face gently. Then he began to massage my hands. As circulation came back, they tingled and I whimpered with the pain and tried to draw them away.

His grip tightened and he went on rubbing. "It won't be long now," he encouraged me, "but we've got to get the blood circulating again." And in a little while the pain subsided, though my fingertips were still tingling. "Now that's better," he said, but he regarded me uneasily. "You ought to see a doctor or I'll get you to the emergency room at a hospital where you can be patched up."

"It isn't necessary. Anyhow, what could I tell them to account for the way I look and what has happened to me?"

"God, when I saw how that burn just grazed your eye! It's a miracle you weren't blinded. And those other burns should have some attention. I hate to think how much they may be hurting you."

"I bought some ointment at a pharmacy, but it's in the Volkswagen, which I left in a parking area at a shopping center. And my hands are all right now."

I managed to stand up with his help, holding the back of the chair for support because the room had an unpleasant tendency to tilt first to one side and then to the other. "I don't deserve having you help me. I put Fred and his mother on your trail. I'm ashamed of myself, but I was so horribly frightened when he threatened to burn out my eyes that I just sold you out to gain a reprieve for myself. How did Fred trick someone like you into coming here?"

"He had nothing to do with it and you needn't worry any more about putting him on my trail. Last night I knew by your expression that you had hit on a course of action, so I was following you this afternoon. In fact, I was parked right behind you at the shopping center when the old woman picked you up in that electric cart."

"But I didn't even see the white Pontiac."

"I knew that you had spotted it, so I rented a Chevrolet."

"But why did you come here? Why were you following me? Were you afraid I'd get away with the money?"

There was a reproachful look on his face that made me feel ashamed, but his voice betrayed no resentment.

"I thought you were getting in beyond your depth and that you might need some help. When you began to scream, I was sure of it. The door has a flimsy lock, thank God! When no one opened it, I broke in. I just had time to see that junkie knock you out when something hit me like a sledge hammer. I woke up at least half an hour before you did and there wasn't a sound and not a sign of life. I thought they had killed you. The best moment of my life was when I heard you begin to stir and moan."

The best moment! That moment of my awakening had been the worst of my life, the moment when I realized that Will was dead. I would have given anything to be able to go back to the time when I had been tormented with worry about him. Because with worry at least there is hope. But when hope is over there is no pain, just emptiness.

"Do you think you can come along now? This isn't a very healthy spot, to say the least, and I don't want you found here."

Apparently he had no intention of calling the police, but whether that was on my account or because it would interfere with his own private purpose I did not know.

"Anyhow," he went on, "I want to get some ointment for those burns and something to disinfect the scratches. God knows what filth you may have picked up on the floor. Then I'll buy you a drink and get you some sort of dinner."

It seemed queer for life to go on just the same and for food to be important.

"I couldn't possibly eat anything," I protested.

"You can't fall apart now. You need food whether you are hungry or not. You still have a big job to do, and it won't get easier."

"I know," I said, "but I can't go anywhere looking like this without starting a riot. Anyhow, I want to search the shack before I do anything else."

"Not now. There's no time for that. The idea is to get the hell out. They may come back with reinforcements."

"Will was here," I said stubbornly. "I want to look. There may be some trace of him, some clue to show what happened. When they come back, they'll make sure there is nothing for us to find. It has to be now."

Ronald started to protest and saw that it would be pointless. Instead, he helped me search as the quickest way of getting me out of there.

In the living room there was nothing to indicate that Will had ever been in the place. Under a pillow on the sagging couch there was a pale pink nightgown and I assumed that Fred's mother slept there. In the bedroom there were two army cots, on one of which lay Will's sports jacket and his sun glasses. Apparently they had served their purpose and Fred did not plan to use them any more. I gathered them up gently because they were all I had left of Will. I felt in the pockets, but they were empty.

Knowing that it was useless to try to persuade me to leave the shack until we had inspected everything, Ronald checked the makeshift wardrobe, behind a frayed curtain, opened the bureau drawers and the medicine cabinet. He began to whistle a monotonous little tune.

"They've certainly made a clean sweep. I wonder what they were afraid of." In the kitchen we found a flashlight which he decided to take along. Aside from dirty dishes and bottles, there was nothing in the kitchen. Apparently food was bought only from day to day. In the refrigerator there were some bottles of beer and, in an open, ill-smelling garbage can there were the containers in which frozen dinners were sold. Leaning against the wall was a rusty spade at which Ronald looked thoughtfully for a moment.

At length he said, almost in relief, "That's all there is. I'm afraid we've drawn a total blank."

"I can't understand it. If Will lived here, he must have left behind some trace. He is—he was the most disorderly—" Hearing my voice break, I stopped talking. I hated to give up and leave the shack, my very last trace of Will, but after a final look around I followed Ronald outside. He began to swear.

"What's wrong?"

"They stole the Chevy and they've taken the electric cart, too. We're going to have to walk until we can find a telephone and call a taxi. No, we can't do that. You are in no shape to walk. I'll go down to the filling station on the corner. Will you be all right?"

"Yes, of course." After all, nothing more could happen to me now. "You go on."

He gave me the flashlight. "I don't like leaving you alone, but you won't want anyone seeing you while you look like that. If anything frightens you, signal with this. I won't take my eyes off the place."

After a long look at me he started off at a trot for the filling station. The temperature had fallen and I was chilly, but I preferred being outside to waiting in that horrible shack. Anyhow, I felt safer outside. I watched Ronald run lightly down the street and go into a lighted glass telephone booth and I began to walk up and down, careful not to stumble over anything. One more fall and I would simply refuse to get up again. I'd lie there and die.

No attempt had been made to mitigate the ugliness and barrenness of the ground. I went around the side of the house where I would be sheltered from the night wind, which seemed to fan my burns, and I switched on the flashlight cautiously, just enough to keep me from falling over anything. Then I noticed to my surprise that, unlike the front of the place, some attempt had been made to fix up the back. Ground cover had been planted. At first I thought someone had planted a flowerbed, and then I felt the jolt at my heart even before my mind had fully grasped what I had seen, the long narrow place in the very middle, just the size of a grave.

"Will!" I was running, stumbling toward the grave, crying aloud. "Oh, Will, love!"

Feet pounded around the house. "Helen! You okay? I couldn't find you and I thought—what on earth? Oh, God in heaven!"

"It's Will," I sobbed. "It's Will."

He took the flashlight out of my unresisting hand. "So that's why they cleared out. I should have guessed. I'll have to get you away from here, Helen. I tried to find a cab but they are all busy and it may be half an hour before we can pick one up. We can't wait that long. We've simply got to walk."

"I'm not going. I've got to know. I've got to." As a rule I am docile to the point of being a rabbit, my natural reaction to the headmistress. But when you really make up your mind about something, people will recognize it and give way.

Ronald saw the unwavering determination in my face, heard it in my voice. This time he was the one to yield. "Okay." He went back into the house to get the spade. When he returned, he said, "I hate like hell to let you go alone but you mustn't stay here. I'll take care of this."

"I'm staying."

He did not argue. "Then hold the light, will you?" While he worked, shoveling the ground cover and dirt to one side, we did not exchange any words. It was a shallow grave. Ronald had been working only a short time when he took the light out of my hand. "Turn your back."

I tried not to listen, but I knew when he knelt and began to brush dirt away with his hand. Then there was silence, broken only by the rattling sound of palm fronds somewhere nearby, as they were stirred by the night wind. At last Ronald moved abruptly. He was being excruciatingly sick. I did not think at all. I was cold and dull and empty.

After a long time the flashlight beam found me and Ronald came to take my arm. "I've got to get you out of here." His voice was almost unrecognizable.

"We can't just leave him," I said despairingly.

"My dear, it won't matter to him now. As soon as I get you safely out of here I'll call the police."

"Ronald, I've got to see him."

"No!" When I continued to pull against the pressure of his hand trying to draw me away, he said, speaking with difficulty, "It's been six months, you know."

At first I did not understand what he meant. Then I screamed.

TEN

I don't remember much about the walk back from that shack, although at the time it seemed interminable. Nothing really registered with me but the knowledge that Will lay in a shallow grave and I had left him there. Half a dozen times Ronald Boyd prevented me from stumbling over a curb or walking blindly into the path of an oncoming car. Neither of us spoke until he steered me into a dark and deserted parking area.

I balked then. "Where are we going?"

"Your car," he explained. "This is where you left it this afternoon."

That afternoon seemed to belong to a different existence, a time when Will was still alive, when he might be around the next corner. A time when anything was still possible.

Ronald took my handbag and fished for the key, helped me in and drove back to the building with its Polynesian setting. It's queer how things get out of proportion. The knowledge of Will's murder had numbed me without causing pain. The knowledge that he would have loved the gay and cheerful setting of the little pink cottage, which he would never see, hurt terribly.

Ronald unlocked my door and made sure the draperies were closed before he risked turning on the lights, in case Marilyn Wilson should be awake and watchful.

I tried to rouse myself then. "What are you going to do about the stolen Chevrolet?"

"Nothing. Someone will find it and turn it in."

"But you should report it. The police will wonder why you didn't. And if Fred drove it away, there might be something, fingerprints maybe. You'd be in trouble if you couldn't explain them."

"You're right. I'll report it at once."

"Will you tell them where you left it?"

"My God, no! I'll tell them it was in one of the big shopping areas." He hesitated for a moment. "Can you undress yourself?" he asked doubtfully.

"Yes, of course. You'll call the police at once, won't you, and tell them about Will? I can't bear thinking of him there. All alone."

"Right away. I'll take care of everything. You go to bed." He went away, closing the door quietly behind him, and I stumbled into the bedroom where I undressed. I had my hand on the light switch when I heard the cottage door open and I called sharply, "Who is it?"

"Ron. And keep your voice down."

"What do you want?"

He came into the bedroom, looked at me in that transparent gown, picked me up and put me on the bed. Then he sat down beside me and opened a jar of ointment, applying it cautiously to the burn on my lower lid so the stuff would not get into my eye, and then to the ones on my throat and arm. "That ought to do the trick. This stuff works fast." Before I could speak, he went out to the kitchen where I heard the heavy door of the refrigerator close. He came back to put a glass in my hand. "Scotch and water."

"I don't want it."

"You'd better drink it." He didn't budge and I realized he would wait all night, if necessary, until I had drunk the stuff. I raised the glass and he went back to the kitchen. In a dim way I wondered what he was doing. Then he returned with a cup and saucer. "Finish that drink."

"I've had all I want."

"Bottoms up. And hurry. This thing is hot."

I looked up at him helplessly but I did as I was told and set the empty glass on the table beside the bed.

"Good girl," he said. "Now take this."

"What is it?"

"Hot soup."

"I'm not hungry; I can't eat."

"Oh, yes, you can." He held a spoonful of soup to my lips. "Open up."

I swallowed the soup and realized that it was good and that I was ravenously hungry. I had had no food in more than twelve hours. I reached for the saucer. "I can feed myself."

"Good." He relinquished the cup and saucer and watched while I drank the soup. What with the drink and the hot soup, I was warm again. "How are the burns?"

"Much better. They don't hurt half as much."

"I'll leave the ointment here on the table beside your bed. Use it again if the pain wakes you up, and be careful about the one under your eye."

"Wakes me! I won't sleep tonight."

"Oh, yes, you will. I dissolved a couple of sleeping pills in your drink."

"Why, you—"

He looked gravely down at me. Then he bent over and brushed his lips lightly over my forehead. "Medal for a brave girl," he said and left me. I heard the cottage door close behind him.

As soon as he was out of sight, I forgot him. I lay staring up at the ceiling, flinging my arm across my eyes as though that could shut out the picture of Will in his narrow grave. Will who had been there all the time. After all, he had not succeeded in escaping from Fitz. Nor, I realized, had I. Fitz had used Fred to spy on me, to put in an appearance when I might be on the point of giving up. It was my decision to surrender the hatbox that had led to that horrible scene at the shack. Apparently Fitz had hoped to keep me docile until it would be safe to put the money in circulation.

At least he knew that he would never be able to lay hands on the money. By now Fred and his horrible mother would have told him so, to justify their failure in getting it. He would know that it was forever out of his reach. Not even torture would help him to gain his ends. I tried to remember whether Fitz had ever known of my close relationship to the Hepburns. Yes, of course he had. Will had been so naïvely proud of going to their beautiful house that he had told Fitz. He would be bound to guess how I had disposed of the money.

Oh, Will! Oh, love! Tears welled up in my eyes. I tried to remember him as I had last seen him and how I had lain in his arms all that night. But the picture blurred and faded, and I fell asleep.

ELEVEN

I must have slept at least twelve hours. It was nearly noon when I was startled awake by the loud backfire of a truck. Sun was pouring in the bedroom window. I was aware of drowsy lassitude and I lay without moving, contented in that state between sleep and waking when the memory of the early morning dreams is more real than the outside world.

When I moved my head on the pillow, I felt the sting of the burns and at once my memory came flooding back, all the horrors of the day before with its hideous culmination in the discovery of Will's grave. I didn't cry any more. The emptiness that was all that was left seemed to numb pain. But I thought of Fitz and Fred and Fred's mother with a savage desire to make them pay and pay and pay for what they had done to my sweet-tempered, gay-hearted, trusting young husband.

Slowly I was roused out of my physical apathy, a result of the unaccustomed sleeping pills and the ordeal of the day before. I had to know what had happened and whether Ronald had kept his word to call the police. Only when I got out of bed and stood swaying dizzily did I catch a glimpse of myself in the mirror and I realized how revealing that diaphanous gown was. Not that it mattered greatly. Ronald was not interested in me as a woman, only as bait to lead him to Fitz, and that kind of bait I was willing to be. He couldn't want to find Fitz any more than I did.

Or did he still believe that I would lead him to the money? He had virtually admitted that he wanted to get his hands on it; he had tried to frighten me by describing the danger I'd be in if I did not surrender it. To him, he had implied. He had, by his own admission, followed me to the shack where Fred waited to torture me. And yet he had taken care of me, cut me away from the chair, brought me safely home, treated my burns with unexpected gentleness, brought me a drink and made me hot soup and made sure that I slept.

A hot shower stung the burns alive and I used more of the soothing and healing ointment on them. Dressing was awkward because my arms and shoulders were stiff from being dragged back so that I could be tied on the chair. When I tried to brush my hair into its usual smooth roll I nearly cried out. There was a lump the size of an egg behind my left ear, so exquisitely painful that I was bathed in a cold sweat. My face was barely recognizable, swollen and discolored; the scratches made angry red streaks, and the burn on my lower lid looked ugly. I did the best I could with cream and powder, but I still looked as though I had tangled with an electric saw.

Automatically I reached for my wig and then I sat staring at my reflection in utter dismay. Ronald had pulled the wig off when he was washing the dirt out of the scratches. I tried to remember what had happened to it. All I was sure of was that I had not put it on again. Then I recalled Ronald dropping the thing on the floor under the table; he must have left it there. When the police found Will's body they would find a woman's blond wig. If I had been wanted for questioning before, I'd be wanted for murder now.

I went into the living room to get my little transistor radio and then decided I needed coffee to fortify me and clear my head before I'd be able to cope. When I had drunk a cup of coffee I sliced an orange, toasted an English muffin, and poured more coffee. I made myself finish every scrap of it. For a few minutes I sat looking out at the pool with the sun on it, seeing the bold line of mountains, and nearby a mockingbird went enthusiastically through his repertory. At last I was ready to turn on the radio.

The announcer was describing a multiple car crash. He went on to speak of a student's demonstration. Then he said briskly, "Last night the body of an unidentified man was found buried in a shallow grave behind a deserted shack. According to the police they received a telephone call from a man who refused to give his name, telling them where to find the body.

"The skull had been crushed by a heavy blunt instrument and he had been dead for some months. There is as yet no clue to the informant, who apparently discovered the grave accidentally, as it was partially uncovered, and a spade was lying beside it.

"The manager of the Brown Shield Taxi Company, who heard the early morning report of the crime on this station, informed the police that a call was received last night from a man who gave no name but asked to be picked up at a filling station on . . ."

The voice faded and came on again. ". . . instructed a driver to pick up a passenger there. When the driver arrived, some thirty minutes later, the night man at the filling station said he had not noticed anyone using the public phone booth at that time. He had been inside the station eating a late supper. He had a vague impression that he had heard a woman scream a short time earlier, but he was not sure. Sometimes there were peacocks around and they sounded like screaming women. He had been mistaken once before.

"The shack on whose grounds the murdered man had been buried was condemned some months ago as unfit for habitation. According to the manager of the filling station, several people had been known to occupy the shack in recent months, apparently as squatters: an elderly woman with white hair who drives an electric cart, a frail-looking boy, and a young man who is rarely seen except at night.

"The only clue was a blond wig which may have been overlooked. A statewide alarm has gone out for the woman and her son. The informant is urged to come forward.

"Today's races..."

I switched off the radio. Will's body had not been identified. Ronald had alerted the police but withheld his name. For a long time I sat staring at the wall. When I finally got up, I had determined on my course of action. What I failed to take into account was Ronald Boyd.

He tapped on the door about two o'clock, calling in a loud and cheerful voice, "Hey, open up there before the frozen stuff gets defrosted."

I opened the door and saw that he was carrying a big bag of groceries. He stepped in briskly, saying, still in that unnecessarily loud and carrying voice, "Here you are, lady. I got everything on your list except the chutney." Then he lowered his voice. "This is the stuff from the Volkswagen and here is your car key. That Wilson woman is suntanning beside the pool and she saw me coming this way."

He put down the shopping bag and stood looking me over. He shook his head. "Not so good. Definitely not so good. There's some stuff on the market that would make you look tanned and at least cover the scratches and disguise most of that discoloration. I'll see what I can find. You'll have to stay out of sight until your face looks a lot better."

"I can manage. Don't bother."

"It's no bother. Anyhow, I owe you that."

"Why?"

"For one thing I blundered and left your wig behind in that shack. Have you heard the news?"

I nodded. "You can't be blamed for that. Anyhow, I don't see how the wig could possibly be traced to me, as you did not identify Will's body. You don't owe me a thing."

"Oh, yes, I do. One of these days you'll know just how much I owe you and you are going to hate my guts." The strain of the night had taken more of a toll on him than I had realized in those moments of shock and grief last night. He looked older and a lot harder than he had the night before. "Well, I had better get out of here before dear Marilyn starts adding two and two and making five. Just keep out of sight. I'll get some suntan lotion and anything you need from the store."

"Thanks, but I can't stay in. I'm going to the police today with everything I know and I'll collect the money and take it with me. Now that I know Will is dead there is no further reason for keeping up this distasteful masquerade."

"There is a reason. Nothing that has happened alters that reason in the least."

"Well?" I didn't mean to sound encouraging and I wasn't.

"Listen to me, Helen." Ronald pushed me gently into a chair and sat down facing me. Judging by his eyes I thought he had not slept at all, but there was in his voice something of the quality it had had the night before when he refused to accept defeat.

"I told you that I was looking for a man. I'm still looking for him but, in order to smoke him out, I need that money as bait. Once he learns that it has been surrendered to the police and that it is out of his reach, he'll go underground and stay there."

"I don't see what you can expect me to do."

"Look, Helen, I know this is hell for you, but do you honestly feel justified in helping that man to escape what he has coming to him, when he has already gone to such terrible lengths to get the money?" Ronald played on me as skillfully as though I were an instrument he had mastered.

"What do you want me to do?"

"Help me bait the trap," he said promptly. "Help me take an evil human being out of circulation. As long as the money is where you can lay your hands on it—"

"I won't tell you where it is. Nothing can make me

tell you where it is, and I'm not going to remain silent and let Will be buried without so much as a name. You are wasting your time, Ronald. I've made up my mind. I'm going and I'm going now."

He did not move. "You are a stubborn little fool, Helen. Very beautiful, though not at your best right now, but a little fool, just the same. I'm not going to let you spoil my game. I'm after a man who has killed three people that I know of, and destroyed other people's lives so that they welcomed death. A criminal who takes what he wants without a moment's thought of its effect on others. Every hour that he is left free he has an opportunity to do more harm in the world. Can't you put aside your own feelings and help me take him out of circulation?" The man's passionate conviction rang in his voice and I found myself shaken.

"Oh, dear, I'm so confused and dazed that I'm not sure about anything any more, except that Fitz must know by now that he can't touch the money. It's in the hands of friends who would never, never relinquish it to anyone unless I agreed, and they aren't people to be tortured or bullied or frightened. They are so protected by all the safeguards that go with wealth that no one can get to them without being thoroughly screened. Fred and his mother knew I was telling the truth, that even if they could force me to give them my friends' name, it wouldn't do them any good. So, don't you see, Ronald, he won't risk coming near me. He'd gain nothing by it."

Ronald was silent for a long time, but not as though he was defeated; rather as though he was gathering his forces for a new attack. I saw how desperately tired he was. For the first time since I had known that Will was gone forever I was conscious of the needs of someone else.

"Have you eaten anything?"

He came back from a long way and looked at me, half puzzled, as though he did not grasp what I was saying. Then he made an impatient gesture. "I had some coffee this morning; I'm not hungry."

"I'm going to fix you some lunch."

"Don't bother."

"Turn and turn about is only fair." I looked through my supplies, opened a can of black bean soup, added sherry, and spread some ham sandwiches. I had to speak to him twice before he came out of his absorption with a start and sat down to the scratch lunch. He disposed of the food quickly, though I doubt if he knew what he was eating. At least, by the time he had finished, he did not look so tired and drained of energy. He got up to clear away his dishes and stack them neatly in the sink.

"Well, Helen?" he asked at length.

"Well?"

"What are you going to do?"

"What do you want me to do?"

He heard the weary capitulation in my voice, put his arm around me and gave me a brotherly sort of hug. "Good girl! Just hold out for a few days. Is that too much to ask? It can't be much longer than that. Now the body has been discovered, he has to act fast and he has to act alone. He can no longer trust Fred and his mother because they know you won't relinquish the money and that he's a man on the lam for a murder rap. They never figured on getting involved in murder, just on laying their dirty paws on easy money. Actually, I don't suppose either of them is mentally capable of thinking more than one move ahead."

"What do you suppose he will do?"

"He has only one choice. He'll make an effort to get in touch with you."

"Oh, no!"

"Don't panic!" he said sharply.

"I'm not panicking."

"He can't hurt you. I'll be keeping an eye on you. That's a promise, Helen."

TWELVE

In the long run I said I would hold off my visit to the police for three days. Not one more minute. "But I can tell you this, Ronald Boyd, you'll be wasting your time. You think if I don't surrender the money you can use it as bait to catch Harry Fitzhugh, but I'm as sure as I am that I am standing here that Marilyn Wilson knew about the stolen money and that she could tell you where to find Fitz if she wanted to."

"You can't be sure."

"She knows who I am. I'm positive about that. When I found her searching this cottage, she practically defied me to complain to Jack Mason, the manager's policeman husband, because she knew I wouldn't dare. I tell you she knows."

"I'll find out. I've been getting some peculiar ideas about Marilyn." He looked at me vaguely. "Thanks for the lunch."

"You're welcome."

He turned back from the door. "How are the burns?"

"Better, thanks. The ointment helps."

"Good." He nodded and went out.

I could hear Marilyn's voice. She must be doing her sunning practically against the wall of my cottage. "Well, well, you seem to be chased by all us girls."

"I know. I'm always having to fight them off. It must be my good-neighbor policy."

"Have you tried the pool yet? It's marvelous today."

"That sounds like just what the doctor ordered. I'll join you in a few minutes."

It wasn't much more than that before I heard Ronald say something and then there was a splash as he dived into the pool. Marilyn stood on the diving board and I realized what a pretty figure she had. She gave Ronald ample time to appreciate it before she dived cleanly, almost without a sound.

I pulled the draperies almost shut. All afternoon I cleaned the cottage, scrubbed the bathroom and kitchen, and waxed the furniture, keeping myself busy. But I couldn't control my thoughts. Now and then I listened to the news and about every third time there would be a recapitulation of the story of the discovery of the body of an unknown man, but no new facts were forthcoming.

Apparently Ronald had accepted my belief that Marilyn Wilson was the link to Fitz. At any rate, for the rest of the afternoon he stayed with her. They alternated between swimming and sunning themselves beside the pool. Several times I heard Ronald's laugh while Marilyn chattered endlessly. They seemed to be on the best of terms and I wondered what on earth they found to talk about, hour after hour.

Only once was any comment made that seemed to have any bearing on the situation. Marilyn exclaimed, "My dear, what on earth have you done with your wrists?"

I couldn't make out Ronald's reply, but she said, "You know, they look almost as though you had been tied up!"

"Darned if they don't," he said easily, and turned on his face to get the sun on his back.

Late in the afternoon the temperature began to drop as usual and Marilyn went into her cottage to dress, while Ronald returned to his own. I had opened the draperies a little, but as long as I did not turn on the lights I could not be seen. Perhaps it is unattractive to spy on the movements of other people, but I was desperately anxious to know what Marilyn really was, why she was here, and how she knew about me. Her arrival at this place had been no accident, but it was difficult to guess what progress Ronald was making in worming his way into her confidence. Their conversation had seemed to be largely flirtatious.

When she came out of her cottage again, she wore long flapping scarlet culottes, a loose yellow shirt that hung over it, and gold sandals. Her hair was piled up so that it looked a foot high and she had put on her artificial lashes and so much make-up it was hard to detect even her real bone structure. She had, I saw in resignation, brought out her guitar.

A few minutes later Ronald joined her. He had changed to well-tailored slacks and a white shirt, open at the neck. Again I had a curious sense of familiarity, as though I had seen him before. He was carrying a pitcher in one hand and a couple of frosted glasses in the other.

"Too early for a martini?" he called.

"Never too early." When he had filled the glasses, she put aside the guitar on which she had been strumming idly and raised her glass. "Happy days."

"Happy hunting," he said idly and I saw her swift, appraising look at him. Then she turned in annoyance as Jill Mason came running toward them, looking like a tall schoolgirl in her blue jeans and shirt.

"Mr. Boyd! Telephone. It's the police."

He set down his glass. "Be right back." It must have been a quarter of an hour before he came back and during that time I had imagined almost every possibility. Beside my cottage he dropped his knife with a clatter, said "Damn!" and bent over to retrieve it. A slip of paper slid under my door.

"The police found the Chevy," he had scrawled on paper torn from a notebook. "They called the renting agency who gave them my name. They identified the fingerprints on the wheel and the car door as those of one Fred Cook, who has a record of petty theft but no convictions. The Chevy's fenders were badly dented, so apparently he was in an accident. If I had not reported the loss of the car I would be in real trouble. One up for you, Ron."

I read the note twice and then tore it up and flushed it down the toilet. Outside I could hear Marilyn's coy comments about people who are wanted by the police and Ronald's casual explanation that he had lost his billfold, which had apparently been picked up by an honest man, as nothing was missing. I could hear his cheerful voice and the rattle of the ice as he poured more cocktails.

At length Marilyn said, "It's getting too chilly for comfort. Come along and we'll finish our martinis inside."

After awhile I reheated the soup I had prepared for Ronald's lunch, but I wasn't hungry. The last time I turned on the radio, there was no mention of Will. The arrest of a former movie star on a charge of drunken driving had supplanted the story. Crime must be served up hot to be palatable.

It was hard to get it into my head that I would never see Will again, never have him take me in his arms. Never. Never.

I undressed slowly and went to bed. Ronald was still in Marilyn's cottage, but tonight the guitar was silent. In fact, so was the cottage.

THIRTEEN

I never heard my door open. What brought me upright in bed was the sound when someone stumbled over the coffee table in front of the couch and muttered a curse. The noise as he fell sounded like thunder to me and must have seemed even worse to the intruder.

Fred! It could only be Fred, come to finish his work on my eyes. I screamed "Help!" at the top of my voice and heard footsteps move across the living room in the dark, but whether going out or coming toward me I could not tell.

I did not dare turn on the bedroom light, but I slipped noiselessly out of bed, groped for slippers, and put on my robe with hands that shook.

"Helen!" That was Ronald banging on the door. He rattled the knob and then flung the door open. "Helen!"

"I'm here." I switched on the bedroom lights and he turned on those in the living room. He wore rumpled pajamas and bedroom slippers.

"What happened?"

"Someone broke in the cottage. He fell over the coffee table and that's what woke me up. It must have been Fred. There's no way a stranger could tell which of the cottages are occupied. I told you Fitz would never give up. It must have been Fred. He's been here before, you know."

"And you scared him away," Ronald said in disgust.

"What would you expect me to do?" I was furious. "Lose both eyes?"

"Miss Brown!" Marilyn called. Without the fantastic hair-do and the artificial lashes, and with a face wiped clean of make-up, she was like a different person. Oddly enough she looked younger and not so hard. She wore tailored pajamas and a plain robe and her hair hung down her back in a thick braid. But most surprisingly, she was holding a small but businesslike revolver. She looked from the pajama-clad Ronald to me in my luscious green velvet robe and her eyebrows went up. "Anything wrong?"

"She thought she had a housebreaker," Ronald said lightly, giving me a warning look.

"Housebreaker!" Jack Mason must have dressed like a fireman, because he wore trousers and a sweater. He, too, held a gun.

"Someone got in the cottage. I heard him fall over the coffee table. I was frightened."

"You probably didn't lock the door and it blew open. There's quite a brisk wind tonight. You have to give the door a good hard pull to make sure it catches. What you heard must have been the sound when it blew open and banged against the wall."

It hadn't been the door; I was sure of that. Anyhow, it was an odd door that could have closed itself, and I had never encountered a door that could swear. But I knew that Ronald was willing me to be silent.

"You are probably right," I agreed meekly. "I am terribly sorry I bothered all of you."

Jack Mason had an engaging smile. "So long as you are all right, that's the main thing." He took a closer look at me. So far, manlike, his attention had been concentrated on the revealing lines of my body as they appeared in that beautifully fitting robe. Now he noticed my swollen and discolored face, the angry scratches, the burn under my eye. I should have had sense enough to prepare myself with a plausible story. Instead, I stood staring at him speechlessly.

Ronald came to the rescue. "This is certainly your

unlucky day." He looked at Mason in amusement. "This is Miss Brown's second call for help. This morning she fell when she was trying to save a small kitten from being run over and the ungrateful beast clawed her. So I offered to do her shopping until she is presentable again."

The young policeman glanced from Ronald to me. He saw Ronald's bruised and swollen wrists and he must have associated them with my battered appearance. He didn't seem so boyish when he had his official look. "You'll have to take better care of yourself, Miss Brown." He turned to Marilyn. "I hope you have a license for that gun, Miss Wilson."

"Of course," she said readily. "If you'll come in, I'll show it to you."

When he had followed her into her cottage and closed the door, I asked, "Do you think he believed your story?"

"Not unless he's a fool, and he doesn't look like a fool. Far from it. But you just stood gaping at him, your mouth opening and closing like a drowning fish, and I had to say something."

"Well," I tried to defend myself, "I couldn't think of anything to say."

"That was obvious. What really happened?"

"It was just as I told you. Someone got in and stumbled over the coffee table. I could hear him swear under his breath. I was sure that it was Fred Cook and I yelled bloody murder."

"You did that all right. Be sure you lock yourself in this time. Now if I don't clear out in a hurry Mason will find a lot more to think about."

"Not," I said tartly, "if he has been noticing your beautiful friendship with Marilyn."

"Which makes me wonder just what kind of story she is dreaming up to account for having that revolver."

But whatever Marilyn told him, Jack Mason had no intention of passing on the information. The door of her cottage opened and we heard him say cheerfully,

"Good night." I could not read the expression on his face. He paused beside Ronald and me and looked sharply from one to the other. "You'll remember to make certain your door is shut tight, Miss Brown."

"I certainly will. And thank you again. Thank you both." I closed the door and made sure that the lock had caught. Then I shoved a chair under the knob.

The sky was already growing light by the time I finally went back to sleep.

FOURTEEN

Next morning Marilyn left the cottage fairly early and she did not return for hours. After she had gone, Ronald, arrived to put a new lock on my door. This time he came openly, as last night's experience had provided him with a legitimate excuse. At the same time he brought me a bottle of lotion to use on my face and neck and arms, which gave my skin a bronzed look but concealed the discoloration. The swelling had gone down and the scratches were beginning to fade. The dark complexion seemed odd to me, but I appeared much less battered and conspicuous, which was all to the good.

When he had tried a key in the lock, Ronald looked me over without any enthusiasm. "How long since you have eaten a decent meal?"

"I don't know," I said indifferently.

"We'll go out to dinner tonight."

"No!"

"Look here, Helen. You can't have it both ways. Do you want to continue hiding here, even when your presence is an open secret and the hiding is pointless, or do you want to smoke out a killer?"

"Put that way—"

"How would you put it? All right, let's take a look at the situation as of now. He tried to get to you last night and you scared him away by sounding off like a screech owl, so he's not going to risk coming here again. Therefore he will have to get in touch with you somewhere else. Right so far?"

"I suppose so."

"You know so. Therefore you are going to come out in the open and give him a chance to talk to you."

I swallowed hard. "All right, I'll do it."

He didn't give me any praise. He just nodded. "I'll pick you up about seven."

Ronald had been right, of course. There was no further point in my masquerade. It was a relief to be able to throw away the cheap make-up and shove the flamboyant clothes I'd been wearing into the back of my closet.

That afternoon I shampooed my hair and applied the suntan lotion to my face and throat and arms. When I dressed for dinner, I selected a favorite white wool dress that had been tailored for me two years before in Hong Kong where the Hepburns had flown me for my vacation. It was starkly simple, with a high collar, and it fitted the way only Hong Kong tailors can make clothes fit. I brushed my hair back in its usual plain line and took my short black satin cape with its scarlet lining. From now on I was going to be Helen Gates.

Will had always loved the simplicity of my clothes. I wondered what he would think if he knew I was going out tonight with only one purpose—to act as bait to trap Harry Fitzhugh, to whom he had been so devoted. I did not dare let myself think of what Will's feelings had been in that last minute of his life when he knew that Fitz was going to kill him.

When Ronald tapped at the door that evening, he stood staring at me. "Well," he said lamely, "well." And after a time he asked, "Shall we go?"

About the last thing I would have expected was that I would ever find myself a voluntary passenger in the white Pontiac. Traffic, as always in southern California, was heavy and it was fast. Ronald was a good driver, but slower and more conservative than I would have expected, and he kept his eyes on the road.

"Any choice of restaurants?" he asked at length.

"There's a place I've been going to fairly often since —that is, for the past six months. The food is excellent and the restaurant is so dark that you are not noticed."

"That ought to make it easy for someone to approach you without being observed. I suppose the idea would be for me to drift away for a while and give our friend a clear field."

"I suppose so," I said in a small voice.

"No one could possibly hurt you in a busy restaurant." He was not particularly sympathetic to my fears. He was driving as slowly as he dared, using his directional signals long before they were needed to indicate every turn. I noticed that he was watching the rear-view mirror.

"What's wrong?" I asked at last.

"Not a thing," he said in a tone of satisfaction. "Someone has been behind us ever since we left home and I'm trying to make it as easy as possible for him to follow."

"Who is it?"

"I don't know. I can't make out. He's very cagey and he keeps about three cars behind us. All I'm sure of is that it's a gray Ford and not a new model."

Ronald parked behind the restaurant. The lot was fairly well filled, which was a relief, because fewer people would be apt to notice us when we went in.

As we started toward the entrance, I turned my ankle on a small rock and lost my balance because I hadn't been wearing high heels for a long time. I pitched forward and a young patrolman caught me and set me squarely on my feet. I said, "Thank you, sir."

Ronald laughed. "Do you say 'sir' to a kid that age?"

"I didn't say it to a kid." I was annoyed. "He embodies the law so far as I am concerned."

"And you respect the law?"

I looked up quickly but there was nothing to read in Ronald's face. "Yes, I respect the law, though you try to make that sound funny. It may not be perfect, but it's all we've got. It's that or chaos. We can improve it but we damned well can't do without it."

"You're a little firebrand, aren't you, as well as a mass of contradictions?"

My favorite corner table was occupied, but there was an empty booth near the back of the room. Ronald ordered cocktails and we took our time over them. As my eyes became adjusted to the dark, I watched the door, looking at everyone who came in.

Unexpectedly Ronald chuckled. "If you could only see yourself! You are acting like a startled fawn." I set down my glass so sharply that it rang on the table and his voice changed. He did not ask, "What is it?" He asked, "Who is it?"

"Marilyn Wilson."

"I'll be damned! Alone?"

"Yes. She has taken a small table across the room and near the entrance so we'll have to pass her when we leave."

"I wouldn't have thought she would do anything so obvious." Over my protest he ordered another round of cocktails. "Try not to let her know you have spotted her."

He launched into an absurd and probably imaginary but hilarious story of an experience he had had in a dark restaurant in New York and I was surprised into laughing as I hadn't laughed for six months. After that he ordered dinner and I discovered that I was really hungry. And we talked. How we talked! Ronald asked about my experiences as a welfare worker, about the people who could be helped and those whom it was useless to help because they would go right on getting deeper and deeper into difficulties. He was careful, however, to keep the conversation away from Will and my marriage, steering it into impersonal channels. I had an odd feeling that he was less concerned with my experiences than in what they revealed about me as a person.

And he asked queer and apparently unrelated questions. Had I ever taken a trip on LSD? Or smoked marijuana cigarettes? Why welfare work? Did I believe that criminals were just sick people? In some way the conversation shifted to education and my background and my family.

"Look," I protested at last, "what on earth is this all about? By this time you know the whole story of my life."

He shook his head. "There's a long way to go yet."

"This," I said firmly, "is the end of the first installment."

"Sorry I've been a pest," he said lightly, but I didn't think he was sorry. "There are some things I have to find out about you, and the best place to do that is in a darkened restaurant where I'm not distracted by seeing you too clearly. You sidetrack a man, you know. Once a man starts looking at you, he forgets everything else." He looked at his watch and gave an exclamation of annoyance. "Sorry, Helen, I have a telephone call to make. Do you mind?"

"Not at all." I watched him walk to the back of the dining room where there were two telephone booths. Then I discovered in some surprise that I had eaten almost everything on my plate. I was going to need all the fortification that the hearty meal could provide because just then the man in the next booth stood up and looked down at me.

"Mrs. Gates!" he exclaimed. "I thought I recognized your voice."

I found myself staring helplessly into the familiar face of John Crothers, who had been Will's boss and was responsible for sparking the search for Will in the first place. Usually his was a broadly smiling face, but it wasn't now. It was startled. He tried to speak naturally.

"Well, well. Long time no see. And just as pretty as ever." Behind that artificial friendliness there was a lurking horror of me. "Who's the boy friend? I kind of got the idea from his voice that I'd met him somewhere."

"You probably have," I said casually. "He's an old friend of Will's. He's pinch-hitting for Will tonight. You may have met him at the apartment."

"Yeah. I guess that's it. Well, you tell Will to get in touch with me. Best salesman I ever had. Be seeing you." He glanced at his check, put down money to cover it, nodded to me, and sauntered toward the telephone booths in the rear of the restaurant.

In a few minutes Ronald returned, dropped a ten-dollar bill on the table, said brusquely, "Come on," and steered me rapidly through the restaurant, practically dragging me along, the black cape dangling over one arm because he hadn't given me time to put it on. We were going so fast that I did not even remember to look for Marilyn as we headed for the door. He unlocked the car, almost pushed me in, and had it moving out of the parking lot and into traffic before I had even snapped shut my safety belt.

"What happened?" We both spoke at once.

"Okay, I'll talk first," he said. "I was in one of the telephone booths back there, keeping the door ajar. I was just marking time and waiting for someone to approach you. I didn't think it would be Marilyn because there would be no sense in her talking to you here when she would have no problem in seeing you at the cottage. Unless she was putting the finger on you, of course. Then I saw this guy stand up and speak to you. He came back to the other telephone booth. Someone had been smoking a cigar in there, which is why I had changed. Anyhow he had to leave the door open in order to breathe. He called the police about a woman they wanted, a Mrs. Will Gates, who was sitting in a booth at the back of the Public House Restaurant. He could make a positive identification because her husband had been his best salesman until he disappeared some months ago, leaving his clothes and his new Cadillac behind, after a hell of a row with Mrs. Gates. She was dining with a man who, she claimed, was an old friend. Crothers suspected he might be the guy who helped in the disappearance of her husband. He hadn't caught much of the conversation, but she was laughing a lot and he was telling her how beautiful she was."

"He really believes I killed Will, or at least that I was a partner to it," I said, dazed. "I saw his face. He looked at me as though I was some sort of monster."

"That, of course," Ronald said coolly, "is what you are supposed to be."

We didn't speak again until we got back. Ronald went along to my cottage, unlocked the door, and went through the whole place, even looking in the clothes closet and under the bed.

"Okay," he said at last, "you're safe for the night."

"It was all for nothing, wasn't it?"

He shrugged. "I'm afraid this is going to spur the search for you. I never thought of encountering an acquaintance of yours. That was stupid of me."

"It's not your fault. All that discourages me is that Fitz did not show up in person. He must be leaving it to Marilyn."

"Hm." That was a noncommittal sound and I told him so.

"I'm a noncommittal man. At least all is not lost. You ate properly for once. You've got to make yourself eat, you know. It won't help to get rundown."

"Why are you so very kind to me?"

"I'm not kind. Someday you will know just how unkind I am and you are going to hate me."

"Why? After all, we are seeking the same thing. I can't believe you would injure me."

"You're a trusting woman, aren't you?"

"You trust me," I pointed out, "and I'm a woman wanted by the police for murder."

He laughed at that. "Somehow you fail to terrify me."

"How long had you been following me before you finally spoke to me, Ronald?"

"Someday I may tell you that."

"And why did you?"

"Because I knew that sooner or later you would lead me right where I wanted to go."

"And I have?"

"Not yet. But you will. You have no choice. I need that money, Helen. I intend to have it. At this point there is no sense in having any misunderstanding between us."

For a while that night there had been a respite from the ugliness; there had been natural, spontaneous talk and laughter, and a feeling that I was once more in a normal world, but Ronald's words canceled all that out.

"There is no misunderstanding," I said, "and there will be no money for you. I promised to give you three days before I go to the police. One of them has already gone."

We were standing close to each other, keeping our voices down so Marilyn could not hear us, if she had trailed us home. Without warning Ronald took me in his arms and he was kissing me, almost fiercely at first, and then with long slow drowsy kisses. Little by little, my treacherous hands that had tried to push him off were clinging to him. When he released me at last, I would have lost my balance if he had not steadied me.

"No!" I said. "No! How can I feel like this about you when it is Will I love?"

FIFTEEN

That night I did not sleep at all. My response to Ronald's love-making horrified me. I hadn't known that I was capable of it. And this for a man who had warned me that I must not trust him, a man who admitted that all he wanted of me was the stolen money. I should have felt utterly ashamed, not because Ronald was deliberately using me to serve his own ends, but because I loved Will and I felt that I had betrayed his memory by responding to Ronald's kisses. I never wanted to see the man again, but I knew that, sooner or later, I would have to come to grips with the knowledge that I had never before suspected the potentialities of my own body.

Then I tried to come to grips with the situation that had grown out of that dinner. John Crothers' expression when he recognized me had been fair warning. By now the police search for me would be intensified. I wondered how Marilyn had reacted to the arrival of the police at the restaurant in search of me and whether she would tell them where I was to be found. In that case, the knock on my door might come at any moment. But on the whole I was fairly sure she would do nothing of the kind. She could have done that in the beginning if she had not believed that it would spoil her game. And only God and Marilyn knew what that was.

All the next day I remained in the cottage. I did not want to see Ronald. Anyhow, I was waiting to discover whether the police or Marilyn would make the next move. I couldn't settle down to anything. I kept the radio on and listened to every single newscast, but there was nothing about Crothers' telephone call to the police and the search for Mrs. Will Gates. I couldn't understand it unless Ronald had lied about Crothers making the call.

It was Marilyn who made the next move. She tapped on my door about four. I pulled the draperies aside to see who was there, prepared to keep the door locked if it should be Ronald.

"Hi, there," she said breezily. "I just got a call from my brother-in-law who wants me to fill in tonight. It's not a fine restaurant, not for gourmets, but it's lively. It caters mostly to kids. I got thinking—why don't you come along? Drinks and dinner as my guest."

I would have refused if she had not added, "You never can tell when you're going to meet some interesting guy. Certainly not by staying out of circulation like this."

She means Fitz, I thought. And what better way for him to encounter me than in some unlikely and out-of-the-way restaurant whose clientele was chiefly youngsters?

If I hesitated, it was only for a moment. Sooner or later the confrontation with Fitz must take place and no one could harm me in a restaurant. I wouldn't risk being alone with him in any circumstances.

"That will be fine. How nice of you."

"Good. Be ready about five-thirty. And," she looked at my smooth hair and the plain blue skirt and sweater I was wearing. "Can't you doll yourself up a bit? I don't mean you aren't good-looking enough to get away with anything, but you'll attract attention if you go like that. Like a schoolteacher. No offense meant."

"I'll do my best."

I dug out a pair of fishnet stockings Will had given me but which I had never worn. I worked hard on my face, removed all the suntan lotion and carefully made blue shadows under my eyes, which at least covered the burn on my lower lid. Then, not having the wig, I let my hair hang down my back where it fell below my waist. As a result of all this effort I looked like a nineteen-year-old who knew all there was to discover about the seamy side of life.

When Marilyn called, she stood inspecting me. At length she said, "You're full of surprises, aren't you, Helen?"

Her car was the gray Ford that had trailed Ronald and me the night before. She was a good driver, faster than I liked but competent. She had put her handbag on the seat between us and once when she turned a corner too fast, I fell against it and knew that she was carrying her revolver.

The restaurant was on a poorly lighted side street and it was nearly filled by the time we arrived. It seemed to be a kind of headquarters for hippies. Few of the patrons were more than twenty. Most of them wore tight faded jeans and loose shirts and their hair hung to the shoulders. Except for the ones who had beards it was hard to tell the sexes apart, which may be one answer to the population explosion. Most of them had bare feet.

Marilyn steered me through the restaurant to a table against the back wall. A man who seemed about forty, with a completely bald head and a big black mustache like a pirate's, nodded to Marilyn.

"Good crowd tonight, but Nora is off again. Get busy."

"This is my girl friend. Helen, this is Peter. Food and drinks on me, Peter. See you later, Helen. Have fun."

The bald-headed pirate looked me over. "What are you drinking?"

"Scotch and water," I said, because that would probably be safest.

He nodded and went over to the bar to give the order.

For the most part the youngsters were quiet. They

had been talking briskly when Marilyn and I came in. Now they were silent, looking me over. When they talked again, it was in low tones, still watching me speculatively as though I represented some danger to them.

I refused another drink when Peter suggested it and looked at the menu. Marilyn had been right about the place. The menu didn't offer much variety: spaghetti, pizza, hot dogs, tacos, fish and chips. I decided on spaghetti, which was surprisingly good, with an excellent sauce, crusty Italian bread, and crisp salad.

Marilyn had changed to a bikini covered with brilliants. It did not appear to interest the customers, as nudity is a drug on the market in southern California. She stopped to ask if I wanted anything else and then she was busy carrying mugs of beer and trays of tacos. There was only one other waitress, a heavy woman who might have been fifty, her hair dyed a bright red. She walked as though her feet hurt her and, because of her weight, the "uniform" seemed more revealing than stark nudity would have been.

Little by little, the hippies lost interest in me though they still kept their voices down. At a large round table a debate was going on; it had plenty of fervor, all that it lacked was any trace of originality of thought. I suppose the radio and television commercials are conditioning people to think in slogans. Heaven knows that's the easiest way.

At one table there was a boy who might have been eighteen, with long curly hair hanging below his shoulders and a scraggly beard. The girl with him couldn't have been much over fourteen. She looked like a zombie and stared at me with eyes that seemed to be practically blind. Something about them reminded me of Fred Cook and I realized that these youngsters were already dope addicts.

There was a curiously furtive atmosphere in the room and a faint alien scent. I wondered whether some, at least, of the hippies were smoking marijuana.

When the rush of serving was over, Peter set a chair in the middle of the room and Marilyn came out, carrying her guitar. For a few moments she strummed idly until the crowd fell silent and then she began to sing a long mournful ditty of social protest. There was a little desultory, scattered applause when she had finished, but she evidently took it for approval and she sang an antiwar song that had a strong rhythm. After the first verse some of the youngsters joined tentatively in the chorus. For a third number she played rock and roll with one of those maddening, repetitious beats, and this time the whole room joined in with a grunting sort of refrain that sounded like "Oh, yeah! Oh, yeah!"

Peter was moving slowly around the room, stopping at each table to talk to the youngsters. I don't know just when I began to realize the oddness of his behavior. Something about the place was awfully wrong. Several times I saw him hand a folded menu to people who had finished their dinners. I was almost sure that Marilyn's brother-in-law was distributing dope of some kind and that she was distracting attention from his movements.

I could remember Ronald Boyd's voice as he told me about his brother Ben who had become an addict. Was this the link between Marilyn and Fitz, that he supplied dope for the hippies?

I wanted to get out of there. What I could not understand was why Marilyn had wanted me to accompany her to this unlikely place. My one hope, that I was going to be able to confront Fitz, was fading. I had looked at everyone in the place but there was no one who resembled him in the least. And then I noticed three or four hippies standing at the bar. As one of them stepped back, I saw Fitz, or at least the upper part of his face. He turned his head. It wasn't Fitz. It was Ronald Boyd. As he came toward me, he passed Marilyn.

"That was very nice," he said.

"Thank you, Mr. Fitzhugh. I'm glad you enjoyed

it." There was malice and amusement in her voice.

"What—?" He had no time to complete his startled question.

Peter, who had stopped for a moment near the entrance and had been looking out, came back in a hurry.

"It's a raid!"

The lines at the corners of Marilyn's eyes crinkled, though she was not smiling. Ronald hauled me out of my chair without ceremony and rushed me through the kitchen, which was misty with steam from the boiling kettles of spaghetti, and where a dull-looking chef, his tall white hat pushed back on his head, was taking a hot pizza out of the oven. He did not even look up.

Ronald practically pushed me out into the alley. Then he stopped short. "Damn!" he said under his breath.

A police car had drawn up at one end of the alley, shutting off any escape in that direction. I started the other way, but his hand tightened on my arm. "No use. They'll have that one closed off, too. This way."

He boosted me over a wall and I dropped down on the other side. In a moment he landed beside me. Together we ran along the wall, crouching low. Then he said, "All right. Slow. Try to breathe easily." He put his arm around me and laughed as we strolled past a police car which had just blocked the other end of the alley.

"Well, will you look at that," he said. "What's up?"

In front of the restaurant there was a Black Maria, the door at the back open, a row of benches on either side. Into this the police were herding the hippies, while a cameraman was taking pictures. Some of the hippies waved cheerfully, some of them called obscenities. Marilyn was arguing with the policeman who held her arm. From her gestures I gathered that she wanted time to dress. The older waitress moved apathetically, paying no attention to the whistles of the crowd that had begun to gather. Obviously arrest was no new experience for her. Peter, his right wrist linked to the left of a policeman, was holding a handkerchief over his face.

As we strolled past, acting like curious bystanders, Marilyn saw us. Her eyes flickered and my heart sank. But she got into the police wagon without any remark or look to betray us.

When we had turned the next corner, I pulled away from Ronald's restraining hand and he released me at once. The Pontiac was parked along the curb on the next street.

When we had moved away from the curb, I turned to him.

"What was that raid about tonight?"

"Dope. Couldn't you tell? There were marijuana cigarettes going around and at least half a dozen of those kids were on heroin."

"I shouldn't think they could afford it."

"They can't, but once get them hooked and you have them where you want them. They'll commit any crime to get the money."

"Do you think Marilyn knew her brother-in-law was peddling dope?"

"If he's her brother-in-law, I am the Chief Justice of the Supreme Court. What in hell made you go to a place like that?"

"In the first place, I didn't know what kind of place it was. In the second place, I thought from something Marilyn said that I might find Fitz there."

"Did she mention him?" Ronald asked sharply.

"No. At least not by name."

"And what in hell made you go anywhere looking like that?"

"I thought it was what Marilyn expected. I don't know why she asked me to go there, but she saw us leave and she didn't tell the police. Look here, who are you?"

"Ronald Boyd Fitzhugh."

"Then it was all a lie about Fitz killing your brother Ben."

"Ben and Harry are both my brothers."

"Three of a kind."

"What do you mean by that?"

"Three men with but a single thought: stolen money."

"Not a single thought, perhaps, but it looms large," he said coolly.

"And which of you killed my husband?"

He did not answer. He was watching his rear-view mirror. At length, after turning corners haphazardly, he said, "There is no one trailing us tonight."

"Who is Marilyn working for?"

"Not me."

"But she knows who you are."

"So I gathered tonight. That's the first hint I've had of it."

"How did she find out? Through Fitz?"

"I could make a pretty good guess. I was careless."

"You realize, don't you, that I have no reason for keeping my promise to you about the police. I'm going to them now."

"Oh, no, you aren't. I need more time."

"More time to make love to me, to soften me up so I'll give you the money? Is that it?" I hadn't been afraid of him before. I was now. His anger was almost a tangible thing. But when he spoke, his voice was as pleasant as usual.

"Helen, somewhere in the dim recesses of your so-called mind some sort of cerebration must go on. You are a woman wanted by the police for the murder of her husband. Let's take a look at the case against you. You had a noisy quarrel, you lied to your husband's boss about him going to work, he disappeared without taking any of his belongings or clothes, not even his new Cadillac, not even his toothbrush. You picked up all your things and closed out your bank accounts. You've been living in disguise and under an assumed name and you have nearly eighty thousand dollars in stolen money in your custody. You have been seen with me, a man who has been tentatively identified as a frequent visitor at your apartment, and who was overheard telling you how beautiful you are and who presumably helped you to do away with your husband. The only so-called proof you could produce would be letters that were printed, so there was not even any handwriting to identify. That's quite a case, Helen."

"But I can produce the money and explain why I have acted as I have."

"Who would believe you?"

"But I never saw you until a few days ago."

"Can you prove that? Could you have convinced your friend John Crothers, who obviously took me for Fitz?"

"I didn't know anyone could be so vile and such an unscrupulous liar. Everything you've said and done has been a lie."

"Not everything."

"Did you just happen to go to that restaurant tonight?"

"Of course not. I was keeping an eye on you. I promised you that I would. I keep my promises."

After a long time I asked, "What do you intend to do?"

"I want you to hold off one more day. Perhaps two. If you do that, we can end this situation. If you don't co-operate with me, I'll see that the police know who you are and where you are. I mean that, Helen. And once you are indicted on a murder charge, there is no bail. You'll wait in jail until you are tried. Even if you get a verdict of 'Not guilty' you'll be a marked woman for life. Do you realize what that would mean?"

I didn't answer.

He gave a short bark of laughter. "Yes, I see that you do. I have too much at stake to give you a break, though God knows I would if I could."

"Who gave the police that snapshot Fitz took of me?"

"I did."

"I thought I couldn't hate anyone more than I do Fitz, but I hate you. How I hate you."

"At least there was no deception. I warned you not to trust me. I warned you that I wasn't being kind. I'm completely crazy about you. I love you so much that it's like pain, but I can't give you a square deal. At any rate, I won't. If you were twice as beautiful as you are, I still wouldn't lift a hand to save you if you get in my way. But this much is true and you can believe it. Hold off until I give you the word, and I'll see that you are in the clear. Act now and act alone and you'll be indicted for murder as sure as God made little green apples."

When he had parked the Pontiac, he walked beside me to my cottage. He did not touch me, but I was as much his prisoner as though I were handcuffed.

"Well?" he asked when I had unlocked my door.

"You don't give me much choice, do you?" I said sullenly.

"No choice at all," he admitted.

For a long moment he stood looking down at me and then he took a swift step forward. I saw his expression and I ran inside and slammed the door shut. Last night I had been in his arms. Tonight I jammed a chair under the door to shut him out.

Ronald Boyd Fitzhugh. That was why he had seemed so hauntingly familiar. Fitz's brother. And I still didn't know whether it had been Ronald or Fitz who had killed my husband. Only that if I did not follow Ronald's orders, I would be arrested for Will's murder.

All night long I kept the bedside light burning.

SIXTEEN

Apparently the raid had been a routine police matter with no particular news value. When I turned on the radio next morning, there was only a brief reference to it. A restaurant frequented largely by hippies had been raided as a result of an anonymous tip to the police that the place was a distributing center for dope. Marijuana cigarettes and a large quantity of heroin were found in the possession of Peter Annuncio, proprietor of the restaurant.

Marilyn came home in midmorning and, to my surprise, she tapped on my door a few minutes later. When I admitted her, she dropped down on the couch.

"I'm sorry, Helen. I didn't mean to get you into anything like that."

"It was nice of you not to give us away when you saw us."

"That was the least I could do."

"When did you—I mean—"

She helped me out. "I had to spend the night in jail but I was released this morning. My lawyer was there bright and early."

"How about your brother-in-law?"

"They got him cold. Bail at thirty thousand dollars so he can cool his heels for a while."

"Did you know he was selling marijuana cigarettes and heroin to those youngsters?"

"You could have knocked me down with a feather,"

she said, and I knew she was lying. "I'm glad you got away. That boy friend of yours is a lot of man."

"He's not my boy friend."

"He gives a damned good imitation," she said.

"Why did you call him Fitzhugh last night?"

"Did I?" Again laugh lines crinkled at the edge of her eyes though her lips were sober. "I can't imagine what I was thinking of."

I shook my head. "I asked him last night and he told me who he was. It wasn't a mistake. How did you know?"

"Look here, Helen, in some ways you're just not with it. The Fitzhugh men aren't nice people for you to know. I don't usually attempt to give advice, not at least when I see something important between two people, as there is between you and Fitzhugh. But he's bad medicine." She broke off as someone tapped on the door and I got up to admit Jill Mason.

"Oh, good!" she exclaimed. "I was looking for both of you." There was something different about her this morning; she seemed to be embarrassed, ill-at-ease, and I wondered whether she knew that we had been involved in a police raid and that Marilyn had spent the night in jail. Perhaps she was going to ask us to leave.

"Jack and I are going to have a barbecue tonight. I'll try to get Mr. Boyd and some other guy and one of the older, retired couples who live in the main building. It's a different generation, but they've known Jack all his life and they enjoy being around young people. Suit you?"

"Mr. Boyd would suit me fine," Marilyn said with a challenging look at me.

"Good! And there's an awfully nice guy, a friend of Jack's named Keith Putnam, for you, Helen."

"If you want to be really nice, let me have the baby for my partner."

Jill laughed. "That would suit him. You certainly made a conquest of my son. Six-thirty? We'll supply beer, but if you want something stronger, you'll have to bring your own. See you. Oh, would you mind bringing your guitar, Marilyn? Everyone would love it."

"I'd be glad to."

"Fine." Jill waved and we heard her running toward Ronald's cottage.

Marilyn got up and stretched. "I've got to get some sleep. I'll see you at the clambake. And I'm sorry I got you involved in that raid. Fitzhugh certainly got you out of there in a hurry." She smothered a yawn. "Lucky that he was on hand. You might almost think he had followed you." She smiled and sauntered back to her own cottage.

It wasn't until evening when I was dressing for the barbecue—black wool slacks, a white shirt, and a thick black sweater to ward off the evening chill—that I discovered my cottage had been searched. My handkerchiefs were under my scarves, my cold cream jar behind my powder and lipstick, the book I had been reading moved from the bedside table to the dresser.

I went through the whole cottage then, closets, cupboards, drawers, shelves. There was a faint impression on the carpet where a chair had been moved. Someone had made a thorough search of the place. But at least no trace of the stolen money had been found and no clue to my real identity. My wedding ring was in the zipper compartment of my handbag along with my credit cards, social security card, driving license as Helen Gates and passport as Helen Brown.

I knew now why Marilyn had wanted me out of the cottage the night before. But who had done the searching? Was it Fitz? And that brought me bolt upright and completely bewildered. Marilyn knew who Ronald was, but he had been stunned when she had addressed him as Fitzhugh. Then what was her relationship with Harry Fitzhugh? Not nice men to know, she had warned me.

I heard Jack and Jill pass the cottage half a dozen times while they carried food and supplies down to the picnic area. I waited until they came by with an older couple: a tall, heavy man, broad-shouldered and erect, with white hair, hard eyes, and a weather-beaten look; and a woman with a gentle face who must have been nearly six feet tall, slim and erect, her white hair cut short, wearing warm slacks and a wool jacket. With them, carrying a carton of beer in each hand, came a young man so nondescript in appearance that he was practically invisible. This time Jill was holding the little boy's hand. A few minutes later Marilyn left her cottage, carrying her guitar. I heard Ronald say, "Can't I take that for you?"

"Sure. That's what men are for. Didn't you know?"

"Beasts of burden? By the way, last night, just before the raid, you called me Fitzhugh. Why?"

"Wouldn't you like to know?"

"Very much."

"Well, here it is, right between the eyes. Fingerprints."

I sat down, clutching my head in my hands, feeling that the world had suddenly turned upside down. Ronald Boyd Fitzhugh was a man with a criminal record. Marilyn must be working, not for Fitz, as I had supposed, but for some law-enforcement agency. The gun she carried, the look on her face when the raid started, the raid she must have engineered, it all held together. But why was she devoting so much time to me?

When I left the cottage, I automatically locked the door, though I knew that someone was able to get in and out as easily as though the place belonged to him.

Behind the bamboo fence back of the cottages there was a thatched hut with tables and benches, flaring lamps, and glowing coals prepared for the barbecue. The extremely tall thin palms of southern California loomed up into the sky from which the last of the light was fading. Jack and his wife were busy preparing chickens, and the little boy was underfoot, trying to see everything that was going on.

I scooped him up and played a game with him,

irate husband, "the girls wore short skirts and bobbed their hair; they drank bootleg gin and smoked cigarettes on the sly, and had casual love affairs before they were married. They were called flappers then and we thought they were sinful."

"At least they weren't dope addicts."

That was when I sat up, aware of the undercurrents. The talk was not as idle as it appeared. There was a purpose behind it. But whether it was directed at Marilyn, who had been involved in the raid, I couldn't tell.

Keith started to refill my glass with beer, and I stopped him. He curled up on the ground at my feet and offered me his cigarette case.

I shook my head. "I don't smoke."

"Cancer scare?"

"I suppose that would weigh if I had ever liked the things."

"Doesn't smoke," he commented. "Doesn't drink, at least not much. No vices?"

"Plenty of them, I suppose."

He dropped his voice and I saw Ronald watching us curiously as though he wondered what we had found to talk about. "Next thing—I always like to clear as I go—are you married or anything?"

"I—no—"

"That's nice to know. Though how you've managed to keep free I can't imagine. Did anyone ever tell you that you look like Princess Grace?"

"Occasionally."

"Are you in movies or on television?"

"No, I'm not at all ambitious."

"Just a woman of mystery," he said idly.

"Don't be absurd!" I hadn't intended to speak so sharply, and he was surprised.

"Oh, no, Jack!" I heard Mrs. Sullivan protest with so much distress in her voice that other conversations broke off. "You're doing so well. You've had those citations and you are in line for promotion, and you're such a good cop. I thought you liked your job."

"I do. That is, I did, but things are different."

"What's so different?" Sullivan was demanding rather belligerently.

"Well, when my Dad was a cop, I was proud of him. But now kids call me Fuzz or Pig. Before they get out of junior high school, they've been told that the police are their worst enemies. I don't want my kid ashamed of me or my uniform. Police brutality? Okay, so there are bad cops. But there are bad guys in everything. People know about our trigger-happy cops but not about the ones who lay their life on the line every day and get gunned down in the course of duty by trigger-happy criminals, or bombarded with rocks and bricks by young punks. We're expected to handle these kids as though we were baby sitters and not enforce the law when they lie down on the street to stop traffic or break windows or burn down school buildings or raid college campuses and destroy books and records they are too stupid or too ignorant to understand. Let a cop kill anyone and the public screams. But how many people know of the number of children destroyed every year by criminal or crazy or indifferent parents?"

"Okay," Sullivan grumbled, "I get the picture, so stop bellyaching. And just how are you going to help matters by throwing up your job?"

"Hey, you stop needling Jack," Jill protested. "You let my husband alone."

"Do you want him to be a quitter, girl?" Sullivan demanded. "You want hippies and gangsters taking over the country?"

"But they won't take over," Ronald said, startling us because he had been so quiet. "Hippies don't want to take anything over. That's half the point about them. In the beginning they were the original 'no' kids, no work, no responsibility, no nothing. Not valuable but at least harmless. They don't like violence or competition. They thought they could withdraw to a simpler world. Useless, perhaps, but harmless. Then the smart guys got hold of them, moved in, put them on dope.

Now they are dangerous because when they are hooked, they become tools."

"And so ugly and sordid," Mrs. Sullivan said. "Those dirty bare feet and unwashed hair."

"There's something attractive to the weak about not doing anything," Ronald said. "Of course we couldn't survive if they made up the majority, but a lot of them are nothing but victims."

"It strikes me," Sullivan said, "that people like you think everyone is a victim."

Ronald smiled. "I don't quite know what you mean by people like me. Anyhow, I don't go that far. I'm no extremist. But there are victims and there are victimizers and there's no punishment severe enough for them."

"That reminds me," Keith said. "Did any of you see about that raid on a hippie restaurant last night?" He was sitting at my feet, his shoulder against my knee, and he must have felt me jerk.

"Actually," Ronald said, "I was there at the time. I had just dropped in for a beer when the raid started and I was lucky enough to get out in time." He nodded to Marilyn. "You probably know more about it than any of us. You entertain there, don't you?"

Marilyn had not expected this direct attack, but she pulled herself together. "Now and then I play the guitar there to entertain the kids, but I never dreamed— Wasn't it awful? When Peter said there was a raid, I couldn't believe it. They seemed to be such nice harmless kids, having a good time without bothering anyone."

"I hope you got away all right." Ronald wasn't going to let her off so easily.

"I had to go to jail, but my lawyer got me out this morning."

"What happened to the owner?" Keith put in. "There are some people I'd like to see shut away for life, and he's one of them."

"He's my brother-in-law, and—well, the fact is, my

sister died several years ago and he remarried, but now and then he gives me a job."

"I hope," Jack said, "he won't persuade you to go back again."

"Never," she said feelingly. "And I must say I think the police handled it very well."

"No brutality?" Jack asked.

She laughed. "No brutality." She picked up her guitar and began to play, singing softly, and effectively ending the conversation.

I had a curious feeling that I had been watching the rehearsal of a play.

Ronald gathered up his bottles and glasses. "I'll get this stuff out of the way."

Keith got up. "I'll help you with it."

Ronald gave him a quick look but made no comment, though it was apparent that he needed no help.

"I'll take a look at the offspring," Jack told his wife, and the three men strolled off, Ronald walking between the other two.

It must have been a quarter of an hour before Jack came back alone. Mrs. Sullivan started the break-up of the party. "We've got to meet an early plane tomorrow. Our granddaughter is coming to visit us. It's been a nice party, Jill. I'm so glad you included us with your young people. And thanks for the music, Marilyn. Jack, will you say good night for us to the other young men?"

In a moment we were all standing up, saying it had been a good party and we enjoyed it. Jill refused my offer to help her clear up and Marilyn strolled back with me.

"The men really fall for you, don't they?" she said when we paused at her door. "You had Keith practically drooling. Quite an interesting evening, wasn't it? Cops to the right of us, cops to the left of us. And such a nice discreet arrest. Extractions painlessly made. No fuss. No shots."

"What on earth are you talking about?"

"Keith. He has cop written all over him. Didn't you see that? And he made a nice quiet arrest. Looks like your boy friend is going out of circulation for a while." She looked amused. "Good night."

SEVENTEEN

For hours I lay sleepless, trying to puzzle out the reason for Ronald's arrest. I wondered whether the party had not been arranged to give Keith an opportunity to sum up Ronald for himself. At least the whole operation had been so smooth that I was sure Jack Mason had been prepared for it.

It seemed to me that I had dozens of questions and no answers at all. Was Marilyn associated with the distributors of dope or was she on the side of the law? Why were Ronald's fingerprints on record? What had he done? Were he and his brother Fitz working together? In that case my only safety lay in refusing to tell him where the stolen money was. He had said he had to have it. He had said he would not give me a break. He had said I would hate him. And he had said he loved me. There had been that electric moment in his arms. Well, there was one thing I knew beyond any doubt. There could never be any friendship between me and Fitz's brother.

It was nearly five o'clock in the morning when I heard Ronald walking toward his cottage, heard the click of his lock, and saw him silhouetted against the light before he shut his door with a sharp slam. Well, at least he was not under arrest. I fell asleep and dreamed of the blue-eyed little boy who kept leaning over the edge of the swimming pool. He fell in and I dived after him, seeking that small body with frantic hands through the pool's length until I was choking from being under water. I woke up with my blanket over my head and tossed it back.

When I slept again, Marilyn was forcing me into a car. The people on the street were blind and deaf and I could not attract their attention. It was like something in a Hitchcock movie.

In the morning I jolted myself awake with a cold shower. My face was almost normal and the burns on my throat and arm were healing. The one under my eye was still painful, but the lump behind my ear had gone down and no longer hurt me so much. On the whole I was over the worst, but, like Hamlet, I felt that I could be bounded in a nutshell and count myself a king of infinite space, were it not that I had bad dreams.

While I was eating breakfast, I switched on the radio and listened to the news of the latest strike, school integration, and a fire that had destroyed a bank.

"An attempt was made early this morning to break into the Burton Hepburn house, which has long been a landmark famous for the beauty of its grounds and its Spanish architecture. According to Mr. Hepburn the household was aroused by the frantic barking of his German police dog. When Mr. Hepburn, his butler, and the head gardener went to learn what was wrong, they found the dog had been stabbed. Bloodstains indicated that the housebreaker must have been bitten when he was interrupted in his attempt to cut the glass in a window in the dining room; apparently the intruder escaped by car.

"Mr. Hepburn said that this was the first time anyone had ever tried to burgle the house. Neither he nor his wife had ever kept any appreciable amount of money there and Mrs. Hepburn's jewelry was in a safe deposit box in her bank when she was not wearing it. The flat silver was kept in a storage vault.

"Mr. Hepburn, whose grandfather founded the Hepburn Carriage Company in the eighties, and whose father converted to the manufacture of trucks, carried on the family business until he retired ten years ago. He endowed the Southside Hospital and his wife sponsors the Southside Child Clinic."

When I became aware of the radio again, it was in the midst of a soap opera and I turned it off. So Fitz had made his move. He had guessed where I had deposited the stolen money. It could not be coincidence that the only time the robbery at the Hepburn house had been attempted was after Fitz knew where the money was. From the beginning I had known that I was unjustified in involving the Hepburns in my problems. Now I was responsible for the killing of their police dog.

After lunch I dressed carefully, covered the burn under my eye as well as I could, and went out to get in the Volkswagen. It had been standing in the sun and the seat was blistering and the wheel so hot I could hardly hold it. After a few minutes, with the windows rolled down and a cool breeze lifting my hair, it was bearable.

For the first time in my memory the big iron gates at the Hepburn entrance were closed and locked. I touched my horn and in a few minutes the head gardener came to peer out.

"It's Mrs. Gates," I called.

He stared at me, his eyes growing wider and wider, and then he turned away and used the little telephone that was set in a small metal box in the wall. When he had put down the telephone, he opened the gates and stepped back to let me drive through.

"I understand you had a burglar last night, Vicente."

"Yes, ma'am." There was no trace of his usual beaming smile, so I realized that it was not the attempted burglary that alarmed Vicente. He had seen the news stories about me and I was what frightened the poor man.

I drove up the blacktop road that curved around the front of the house. By the time I'd got out of the car, the butler had opened the door. There was the same look on his face that I had seen on that of Vicente.

"Is Mrs. Hepburn home?"

"You're to come to the library. She said it was all right to let you in." Wilkins realized belatedly that this was not a felicitous expression.

"Is she busy?"

"She is dictating to her secretary."

Mrs. Hepburn was sitting at a businesslike desk going through the appeals for help that form a large bulk of the mail of the wealthy. She turned to give me a long clear scrutiny and I could see her relief when she found that I looked like myself once more. She was also aware of the butler's reluctance to have me in the house.

"That's all, Wilkins," she said, and he went out of the room with a dubious look at me. "We'll do the rest of it later, Miss Field." When the secretary had gone, she held out both hands. And then, to my surprise, because she was not a demonstrative woman, she put her arms around me. "Helen," she said, and there were tears in her eyes. "Helen." Then she sat back, took off her pince-nez to wipe them, and smiled at me. "At last! It's been a long anxious time, my dear."

"I couldn't come before. There were—reasons."

"Burton and I can both read," she said dryly. "We've been following your career in the news. We couldn't understand why you didn't come directly to us, because you must have known that you could count on us. But I won't scold you because at least you are here now."

"I had to come. I'm afraid I am responsible for that attempted burglary last night and I'm so ashamed that I involved you."

"Involved us in what?"

"Do you remember that hatbox I left with you?"

"Of course. Burton put it down in the storage vault. That's what you wanted, isn't it?"

"That hatbox contains eighty thousand dollars in stolen money," I told her.

II

It was not until Mrs. Hepburn had sent for her husband, an order that obviously relieved Wilkins, and asked for some sherry, that she would allow me to talk.

Mr. Hepburn was a quiet man with a dry manner of speaking and a penchant for quotation, not because he was incapable of producing telling lines of his own, but because books were his beloved companions. He had been out to buy another watchdog, he said. His attitude toward me was as casual as though he entertained women wanted by the police every day.

"You are as jumpy as a pea on a hot griddle, Helen," he commented. "Can you not cleanse the stuffed bosom of the perilous stuff which weighs upon it?"

"My dear!" Mrs. Hepburn expostulated.

"I'm just touching the poetic chord," he explained, and I knew that he was trying to make things easy for me.

I didn't know where to start and I finally began with my first meeting with Will at the welfare agency where he had come to help a young delinquent get a fresh start. I told them about our marriage and how happy we were, the only flaw being Will's loyalty to Harry Fitzhugh. And I came at last to the hijacking of the payroll by Fitz, who had shot and killed the armed guard.

I saw Mrs. Hepburn's hand close hard on the carved arm of her chair, saw her startled look at her husband, but she did not interrupt. Mr. Hepburn had kept his eyes on me in an unswerving stare, but his face revealed nothing of his thoughts. "Go on, my dear."

Trying to explain why Will and I had not returned the stolen money immediately and why I had made the Hepburns the unwitting custodians of the money was the hardest part. In fact, until I tried to justify my action in involving them with the stolen money, I had not realized quite how inexcusable it was.

"Will was afraid that Fitz would harm me, as he had threatened. But he never expected that I would be responsible for the money beyond a few days or that we would have to be separated so long. I am horribly sorry and bitterly ashamed."

"Oh, my dear," Mrs. Hepburn began and stopped when her husband made a swift gesture.

"Go on," he told me.

I went on to the six months of hiding and moving on, with those three brief appearances of Will and his letters. Then the man Boyd had showed up, the man who knew who I was, and I had put the ad in the paper, telling Will that I had come to the end of my rope and I was going to take the hatbox to the police.

"You are leaving out things," Mrs. Hepburn complained, ignoring her husband's attempt to silence her. "The pictures of you, the story that you were wanted for questioning, the implications that your husband had been murdered with your connivance."

So I went back to fill in the story, explaining why Will had left everything behind, and how his boss John Crothers had told the police that Will had disappeared after a quarrel with me, and losing a big commission.

Mr. Hepburn grunted and refilled his sherry glass. "Go on."

I picked up the story which was getting more and more painful. Fred Cook's mother had taken me to the shack where she claimed they had looked after Will for six months. I described what had happened to me there: the torture, the arrival of Boyd, and the discovery of Will's body in the narrow grave behind the house.

"That man!" Mrs. Hepburn exclaimed. "The one in the news stories. That was your husband? Oh, my dear!" And this time she came to put her arms around me and press my head against her breast.

"Don't," I said, releasing myself, "or I'll cry. And I don't want to do that."

So I finished the story, telling about Marilyn who, I had supposed, was working for Fitz and who knew me; about Ronald getting me away from the raid at the hippie restaurant, and how Marilyn had called him Fitzhugh. He had admitted that Ben and Harry were his brothers. Marilyn had warned me that the Fitzhugh men were not nice to know. The position of Ronald was the most perplexing thing. At first I had thought he was looking for Fitz, because of his brother's murder, and then that he was after the money, and he threatened that I would be arrested for Will's murder if I did not play along.

"Then this morning I heard about your burglar and I knew Fitz must be looking for the money. He would have guessed you were the only friends I dared trust with it. So I came to say that I am sorry and I'll take it with me."

"Burton," Mrs. Hepburn protested, "we can't let her do that."

"Why can't we?" I had never heard his voice like that before.

"But she—could they arrest Helen?"

He shrugged. "They certainly have every right to question her."

"We can't just stand back and not help her."

"It seems to me that by keeping stolen money in our possession we have done a great deal to help her."

There was no mistaking his tone now. I got up. "Thank you for the sherry and for all your kindness. There is no use repeating that I am sorry I involved you in this ugly mess. If you'll give me the hatbox, I'll take it with me now."

I doubt if Mr. Hepburn had ever remained seated before when a woman guest stood in his presence. But, of course, he did not regard me as a woman guest, let alone as a friend. I was a woman wanted by the police, a woman who had deceived him into acting as custodian for stolen money, a woman who was responsible for the stabbing of his police dog.

"Sit down, Helen, and listen to reason. At least one person knows where the money is and has already made an attempt to get it. If you were that person, what would you do next?"

"I don't know."

"For God's sake," he said irritably, "think!"

"I suppose he would watch this house, knowing that sooner or later I would come here to collect the money and take it back where it belongs."

"So?"

"What do you mean?"

"So what will happen when you walk out of here with the hatbox?"

"Oh!"

"Exactly. I wouldn't give a lead nickel for your life if you try that by yourself."

"Burton!" Mrs. Hepburn cried.

"There's no point in softening the picture."

"Then what am I to do?" I asked.

"Leave this to me. I'll get in touch with the proper authorities and arrange for the right sort of security measures so that when you come for the hatbox tomorrow you will be fully protected. On second thought, perhaps I had better turn the money in myself."

"But that will get you in trouble. No, I'll have to handle it."

"All right. But there will be someone to protect you."

"I—thank you. Oh, thank you! You are so much kinder than I deserve."

"Better, or who of us would 'scape hanging?"

"You're having quite a Shakespearean day, Burton," Mrs. Hepburn said, but she sounded happier and more relaxed. Like me, she knew that he could be depended on to see me through.

EIGHTEEN

Mr. Hepburn accompanied me to the door and I wasn't sure whether he did it to reassure his servants or to prevent his wife from giving me further aid and comfort.

Vicente was hovering near the gates and he closed and locked them behind me with an air of relief. As I put the car in gear, I saw the three-wheeled electric cart move away from the curb, saw the disheveled white wig, and knew that Fred's mother had come to see whether I left the house with the hatbox or empty-handed. If I had been grateful to Mr. Hepburn for letting me wait a day before I removed the money, I was doubly grateful now.

If the money was to be restored to its rightful owners tomorrow, this would be my last chance to find Fitz, so I made a U-turn and followed the cart. This was child's play, as it was moving at not more than ten to fifteen miles an hour. I was held up at a stop light and watched helplessly while a truck and a half dozen passenger cars came between me and the cart.

When the light changed, a pick-up truck turned fast into my lane, nearly clipping off my left fender, and I had to brake. At first I was only half aware of what I had seen, the electric cart parked at the curb. Again I was stopped by a light, but I was in the wrong lane for a turn. While I was weighing my chances of making an illegal turn without being caught at it, the door on the passenger's side of the Volkswagen opened and the old woman got in beside me.

"Keep going. I'll tell you where." I nearly rammed the car ahead of me because the voice, though it was blurred, was Will's voice. "It's all right, darling," he said jubilantly. "It's all right, love."

"Will! Oh, Will!"

"Hey, watch it, love. Look where you are going!" The car swerved dangerously when I turned to stare incredulously at the familiar face under the white wig, familiar except for the red nose and puffy eyes. The latter was accounted for when he pulled out his handkerchief and blew his nose. "Sorry to expose you to my cold germs. My rotten luck. I've not even kissed you in six months and I don't dare to do it now. I'd give you the granddaddy of all colds. But it won't be long. As soon as you can pick up the money, we'll leave for Las Vegas. I made reservations there several days ago. Then, when I've seen a man at Vegas, we can fly on to Mexico City. A private plane. It's all set up. A marvelous climate. A wonderful life for me and my love."

The Volkswagen was under control now and I was driving carefully, watching traffic, an automaton. The blinding realization of the truth had shocked me into the dazed woman who could drive safely but could not think.

After a moment Will said, "Darling, you haven't even said you are glad that I am alive. Remember me, beautiful? I'm your husband and I have come back."

I couldn't answer. I couldn't speak at all.

"Right now, of course, you are surprised."

"Surprised!"

After an interval, he said flatly, "It isn't going to work, is it?"

"No, it isn't going to work."

"You bitched things up, Helen. Why couldn't you have done as I asked you to? If you had kept the money, we would be in the clear now. Instead, you had to turn it over to the Hepburns. I guessed that was what you had done with it. Do they know what is in that hatbox?"

"No," I lied, "just that it was something I was leaving for safekeeping."

"What did you tell them, Helen? They must have seen and heard the stories about you. What did you tell them about me?"

"I said I couldn't tell them anything. Not now. That there were reasons—" My voice trailed off. I've always been a rotten liar; I can't think of convincing stories quickly enough.

"Did you assure them that you hadn't murdered me?" Will sounded amused.

"I didn't need to. They would never have believed it and they didn't ask."

"We'll go back there now so you can get the hatbox from them."

The clock on an insurance building provided the way out. "Mr. Hepburn put it in his bank and it's after three. I'm to get it tomorrow, as soon as he can withdraw it."

"Make sure you do, Helen. This has been too costly an operation as it is. I don't want any more hang-ups. And though you are obviously having a bad attack of rectitude right now, you'll be happy down in Mexico City. I have a ninety-nine-year lease on a wonderful house there; got it over a year and a half ago under another name. We'll be safe and happy."

"Did you get it with the proceeds of another payroll holdup?"

"You've got it all figured out, haven't you?"

I shook my head. "I'm so numb with shock that I can't think at all. The world turned upside down. And you are a stranger I never knew at all."

"You love me, Helen. That can't change. You love me and I love you. When we're together again, you are going to forget all this and be happy again."

"You really believe that, don't you?" I said in a wondering tone.

"Yes, I believe that."

"Will, who is in that grave?"

"I never meant you to see that, love. I never intended to have you involved with that shack or with Fred and his mother, but when Fred came back without the locker key, I figured he had double-crossed me. After all, you can't trust a junkie. So I taught him a lesson in obedience and then his mother brought you there to hit back at me for belting Fred. She figured that if the grave was found, I would have to give them a bigger cut of the money to keep them from talking. That's when I realized from what you said how you had disposed of the money. You had disobeyed my orders and turned it over to the Hepburns."

"Then you were there at the shack?"

"I was ducking around until I could find out what the hell they were up to."

"You were there when Fred burned me with his cigarette and threatened to blind me?"

He was silent.

"You—it was you who knocked out Ronald."

"Is that the guy who tangled with Fred?"

"Yes."

"Why was he chasing you around?"

I did not answer that. "Who is in the grave, Will?"

"Fitz. Didn't your friend tell you? I gather he's the one who found the grave."

"You killed Fitz." My voice was flat. I had no feeling at all.

"Look here, Helen, you were right about Fitz all along. He was no damned good. He worked his way into my friendship and told me all about his company and led up to the idea of hijacking the payroll. We set it up together. When I think how I trusted that double-crossing bastard! Well, Fitz had worked it out with his company and laid a trap for me. The regular messenger had been replaced by an armed guard and he pulled out his gun. I was keyed up. I always am during a big operation. Well, I shot him. I suppose I'd have had to kill him anyhow because he could identify me.

"Looking back I can see just how Fitz worked it. There had been a lot of concern over the payroll robberies I'd pulled off in the past year and a half. That's why Fitz's company co-operated with him. Then, as an extra precaution, they had the money marked.

"I knew that Fitz had set me up and I told him that I would kill him for that. He said it wouldn't do me any good. He had put the whole thing on record, play by play, and I'd never get away with it. He'd been tracking me down because a kid brother of his had worked with me on a previous operation. So he was out to get me. Well, I was so damned mad that I hit him with a shovel and smashed his skull. Next morning I made Fred help me bury the guy. I wanted him so involved that he wouldn't be able to back out."

"What about Fitz's company? Didn't he tell them who you were?"

"That's been driving me nuts. If they know who I am, I can't figure why they haven't moved against me."

"They couldn't, could they, when you disappeared in such a way you appeared to have been murdered by me? You were safe because you were dead. But that means you'll have to stay dead." I found myself laughing.

Will said sharply, "Keep moving. And don't attract any attention. Sure you are upset now. I can't blame you for that. But, except for taking the money to the Hepburns instead of keeping it available, you've been a doll. A real doll, Helen. Together we are going places."

There was a traffic patrolman on the corner. If I could only find some way to attract his attention! I moved into the right-hand lane with its sign: Right Lane MUST Turn Right. If I went straight ahead, he'd have to stop me.

"Turn!" Will said sharply, and there was a gun in his hand. "No tricks, lady!"

I turned the corner. Maybe it would be wiser to wait. Sooner or later I'd run out of gas; I hadn't had the tank filled in days; or something would happen, the "something" beyond reason or probability that is always going to intervene and so rarely does.

"Why did you marry me, Will?"

"Because you're lovely and I fell in love with you. Give me credit, love. I never meant you to know anything about all this."

"Why didn't you keep the money in the first place? Why turn it over to me?"

"I had to get away fast and I didn't dare get caught with the money. Everything went wrong. This is the first job which I ever handled alone. Usually I work with a kid."

"A kid you had put on heroin."

"Right the first time. And it worked. After all, look at it this way. The kids get something they want. But definitely. They love it. And there was never any hang-up until this job, which was jinxed from the beginning. I had intended to use Fred, but he'd gone on a trip with LSD. So I had to do it alone. Then I had to kill the guard. Then I had to kill Fitz. And all for nothing. The money was marked. When I tried to get hold of a good discount man, I found he'd had a heart attack and died. So I had to mark time until I could find a guy who wouldn't cheat me out of my back teeth. I can tell you I was damned rattled that day."

"Only two murders and a robbery that backfired? Such little things to upset you."

"Leave us not have any wisecracks, beautiful."

"So rattled you were able to think out a second line of defense. You set it up to look as though I had killed you. Everything you had was left behind and all my money withdrawn and my clothes gone. The apartment looking as though I had rushed out in flight. Were you pleased when you saw the picture of me and knew that I was suspected by the police of your murder?"

He started to speak and then he began to cough, a

deep rasping cough that shook his whole body. At last he leaned back, wiping his wet forehead, fighting for breath.

"Have you seen a doctor about that cough?"

He gave a strangled laugh. "Still the same sweet Helen! No, love, I have not seen a doctor. And I might point out that I wouldn't have caught this cold if you hadn't lost your head and screamed like a wild peacock when I came to your cottage night before last."

"That was you? I thought—" I shook my head in bewilderment.

Will laughed. "I'll bet you thought it was Fitz."

It was as though a light had gone on in a dark room and I could see things at last as they really were. All along it had been Will who was the thief, the destroyer of young boys, the killer, and Fitz had tracked him down to punish him for Ben's murder, and reported to his older brother Ronald, who had known the truth from the start. It was his brother whom he had found in that narrow grave. He had been stalking me in order to find Will.

Will for whom I had mourned was sitting beside me wearing a woman's white wig and dress. He was holding a revolver in his hand. He sneezed violently and the revolver jerked.

"Where did you go? I don't see how you managed to get away from the cottage without being caught."

"With that policeman between me and the entrance I was trapped. I dropped into the pool and stayed there until the excitement was over. And it got damned cold. Who was the woman with the gun?"

"Marilyn Wilson. I thought— Oh, God, I can't get things straight. I thought at first she was working with Fitz to get the money. But now I think she engineered a raid at a hippie restaurant the other night where the owner was peddling marijuana cigarettes and heroin to the kids. She knows who I am."

"Narcotics Division, most likely. They must be on to me and hope you'll lead them to me. Probably they've found some of the kids I used. Or Fitz really spread the word around. That's why—" Will's voice shook with anger. "You know, just at the moment when Fitz knew I was going to kill him, he laughed. He laughed! He was so sure he had me sewed up."

Will leaned forward and craned up at the sky. "A lot of helicopters around this afternoon. There ought to be a law against them flying so low."

With my world in ashes I was surprised to find that I was fighting back laughter. Will with his virtuous and outraged demand for more law! And with that upsurge of laughter the numbness and shock in my mind dissolved and I began to think more clearly. I had been watching the cars behind me. For once I was hoping to see Ronald's Pontiac—for, after all, he had promised—but it was not in sight. A Volkswagen pulled in behind me and I remembered the coatless man at the wheel whom I had noticed because he was one of those drivers who uses only his right hand, holding the top of the wheel. Once before he had passed me and another time he had driven parallel to me.

"You were the Hepburns' housebreaker last night, weren't you? Did you have to kill the dog?"

"The damned brute raised the whole house and then he bit me. I might have got lockjaw."

"So you stabbed him."

"Baby, when you've got a hundred pounds of dog attacking you, you've got to defend yourself."

The Volkswagen had dropped back and a blue Ford moved into the middle lane right behind me. I had seen the Ford before, too, and the bald-headed man at the wheel. Of course you can pass the same cars for blocks, but I could not help hoping that I was being followed.

Again a helicopter came in, flying low, hovering. Will was watching it, whistling softly between his teeth. "Turn right at the next corner," he said sharply, and I did so. After a few blocks he directed me to go west.

The Ford had come up in the fast lane on my left. When I had gone another block, the Volkswagen was directly behind me.

"Go north at the next light," Will directed, and the Ford dropped back while a pick-up truck followed me as closely as though I were towing it.

"That helicopter keeps coming and hovering over us, no matter where we turn," Will said. "I don't like it."

"How could it follow us? How can anyone distinguish one Volkswagen from another from the air?"

"There are ways. A line of paint on the roof, for instance. We're going to have to shack up at your cottage until tomorrow when we pick up the money."

"But no one can be after you. People think that you are dead."

"That's what they'll go on thinking, with any luck."

"Will, you have left me without much reputation, but I can hardly take you to my cottage."

"I'm your aunt, a harmless little old woman. Where's the scandal in that?"

"You can't go there. The manager is a policeman's wife. And there's a retired police inspector, an old friend of the Masons, who lives in the main building."

"Not to mention the woman who carries a gun. Well, you'll just have to be very, very careful, my dear."

"If you think you can get to my cottage without Marilyn seeing you, you are really mad."

"Marilyn!" Will considered the matter and shrugged off the risks. "Sometimes you've got to take a chance, and there's no place that would be safer. Anyhow, you are going to be mighty careful not to arouse any suspicion. Who's the guy I slugged when he broke in at the shack?"

"His name is Boyd," I said evenly.

"You told Fred he had the locker key and there wasn't one, was there?"

"Fred was going to blind me. I had to tell him something."

"And Boyd followed you to the shack. Why?" Will shook my arm. "Why?" he repeated. "While I was in that damned pool I heard him accounting for those marks on your face, leaping to your rescue as though he had some right. You didn't sound like strangers to me. He—the way he talked—"

"Not as though he was in love with me."

"Well, people aren't that familiar for nothing. If you've been shacking up with him—"

"Stop it," I said angrily. Will's hand on my arm was dry and burning hot. "You must have an awfully high fever, Will."

He released my arm and laughed. "You are incredible! No matter what happens, you can't have people sick or in trouble without trying to help them. No wonder I adore you. So beautiful and glamorous, but at heart you are just a nice ordinary housewife. Or are you, Helen? Do you have potentialities I haven't discovered? I've always wondered if you were really a sleeping beauty whom I'd failed to awaken. Well, there will be lots of time in Mexico to explore the situation."

And then for the first time I was afraid of Will. When I thought of how I had lain in his arms the night before he left me, I was cold and sick. He had come to me after murdering two men. He had left me next morning to bury one of his victims. He had listened without intervention when Fred tortured me and threatened me with blindness. The man I had married. The man I had loved was the man whom Ronald had been pursuing relentlessly. Will had killed both of Ronald's brothers: the young Ben whom he had turned into an addict; Harry, who had trailed him down and died for it. Now Ronald was on his track and he would never give up. I could understand Ronald's horrible nausea when he had uncovered his dead brother's face.

Now I knew why he was determined to prevent me from turning in the stolen money. Once it was out of reach, Will would never risk turning up again. I felt as though some tremendous weight had been lifted off my chest. Ronald was all right. He was bound to be. I wished with all my heart that I had not spoken to him as I had, had not spoken of his dead brothers as I had.

"All right," Will said at last, when the helicopter had gone out of sight, "we're going to your cottage and not a sign to anyone. Is that clear?"

I nodded. I did not want to be shut in the cottage alone with Will, but I had no choice. His revolver was jammed against my side and I drove to the entrance of the apartment building. While I was locking the car door, I saw the blue Ford pass me and turn the corner. Then I started over the little bridge with Will close behind me. In a woman's dress, his feet looked enormous and his knees seemed knobby. The white wig added a touch of the incongruous. His eyes and nose were red and streaming and his face was half covered by his handkerchief. This was Will Gates, thief and murderer, and he looked ridiculous.

He saw the mockery in my face and for a moment something changed in his. I was seeing him as Fitz must have seen him in the moment before his skull had been cracked.

NINETEEN

As usual the door marked MANAGER stood wide open. I could hear Jill's voice as she talked over the telephone and the baby being clamorous about something. If Jack Mason had been home, I'd have risked anything to call him. But his police car had not been at the curb.

As we reached the door, little Johnny came streaking out, stark naked, and ran toward the pool. He slipped in a little puddle of water that had been splashed up. There was a moment of floundering and then he toppled over into the pool. I kicked off my shoes and went in after him, snatched up the slippery little body and came slowly up the steps, my skirt clinging to me.

Johnny howled and I sat down beside the pool with him on my lap and tried to quiet him, to make him laugh. And then Jill came running.

"Is he hurt?"

"No, he's fine," I assured her. "He tumbled in, but there's nothing wrong except that he's scared, and we can't have that." I had stopped his tears by now and I went back to the top step, not regarding the small frantic hands that clutched at my neck. I sat down, talking and laughing all the time, with him on my lap. Little by little I dangled his feet in the water so they made a lovely splash. It must have taken me some minutes to persuade him to lie confidently on his back and float with my hands supporting him. Then I climbed out again and restored him to his mother.

"I can't thank you enough," she said. "This is the second time you've come to Johnny's rescue."

"He's all right now. I just didn't want him to be frightened of water."

"You are absolutely wonderful. And you've ruined your pretty dress."

"Not at all; it washes," I lied.

"At least you'll come in so I can dry and press it for you."

"I'm so sorry I couldn't watch the baby for you this morning, Jill," I said. She looked at me blankly. "But I had to go get my aunt." I tried to hold her eyes. "I had to," I repeated slowly. I didn't dare say anything more. "Heavens, I'm keeping her waiting and she won't like that. Not a bit. I'll have to go."

I did so and unlocked the door of the cottage. Will went inside. He checked to make sure that the draperies were drawn and then he tossed the wig on the coffee table. His hair had been dyed a dark brown. In that woman's dress he looked absurd.

For a moment I stood dripping on the carpet. He took hold of my arm. "That was a damned fool thing to do, taking a chance on the girl getting a good look at me."

"She wasn't interested in you. All she cared about was the little boy. And just what did you think I'd do? Let the child drown?"

"You didn't need to stay there until you'd made him an Olympic swimming champion."

"I didn't want him to be afraid."

"Just one more thing that went wrong. I don't suppose you have a drink in the place."

"Nothing but sherry. But as soon as I can get into some dry clothes I'll get whatever you want. There is a liquor store in the shopping center just a block away."

Will laughed. "Oh, no, you don't. You're staying right here."

"I've got to get out of these wet clothes and take a hot shower."

For a moment I thought he was going to refuse. Then he looked through the little cottage and saw for himself that there was no telephone and no possible way I could get out except by the door. I took dry clothes from the closet and locked myself in the bathroom, where I showered and rubbed myself into a glow and put on the dry clothing. My wet hair I toweled as well as I could and then let it hang loose to dry. This might be the only time I would have to be alone, and I dropped down on a slipper chair to try to think about what could be done.

I had no illusions about Will. Once I had caught a clear view of Mr. Hyde I would never again see him as Dr. Jekyll. I did not even feel any grief for my lost husband. There was a stranger here whom I had never seen before.

I felt sure that I would be safe until we went to pick up the hatbox from Mr. Hepburn in the morning. The arrangements that he was probably making now for my protection would boomerang. When Will learned that some sort of guard had been provided for my protection and not only that the money was out of his reach forever but that he was going to be picked up for multiple murder, he would have nothing to lose. He would kill me without hesitation as he had killed the guard who had threatened, and Ben who would have told the police about him, and Harry Fitzhugh who had trapped him. A man who would have let a baby drown to avoid attracting attention to himself.

I tried to think of what I could do. I had no illusions about my situation. Mr. Hepburn had seen it clearly. It was maddening to have failed to give Jill a message she could understand. She was still within reach of my voice but help could not reach me as fast as a bullet or a knife. I wondered whether Marilyn and Ronald were both away, just when I needed them. There must be something I could do.

At last I unlocked the bathroom door and went out. Will had found the bottle of sherry and he had set a couple of glasses on the coffee table in front of the couch on which he was sitting. He tilted back his glass, drained it, and refilled it.

"Have some." He gestured toward the second glass and the vacant place beside him on the couch.

"No, thanks."

"Have some," he repeated, his expression ugly, and I went to sit beside him on the couch and to raise my glass.

"To the future," he said and began to cough.

Now, when I looked at him closely, I realized that he was really ill. He had a high fever and a racking cough. His eyes were glazed and his nose puffy and inflamed. I tried to find some vestige of the man I had loved, but there wasn't a trace. Then in spite of myself my eyes traveled down the woman's dress and the masculine legs.

"Having fun, love?" Will asked. "Thinking I look kind of comic, maybe?"

"I'm thinking that if you don't see a doctor in a hurry, you will probably have pneumonia."

"That's your fault, you know. If you had carried out my instructions, Fred would have brought me the key, I'd have the hatbox, and there would be no trouble. But you gave it to the Hepburns and jinxed the works. Then you saw the shack and found the grave. You shouldn't have been put through that. Then you got yourself burned. Then when I came here you sounded off and I had to lie in that damned pool and get soaked to the skin. It was all your fault. What in hell did you think would happen to you that made you raise the alarm and bring the cop, the dame with the gun, and your boy friend running?"

"He isn't my boy friend," I said sharply.

"Probably not. You are the original ice maiden. Beautiful but frozen. What did you think you were doing? Protecting your virtue?"

"I thought you were Fred, who had been sent by

Fitz. I thought—all along I thought that Fitz was the criminal, the killer, the thief, the man who taught boys to use drugs and then had them take his risks."

"You have a vicious tongue."

"What in God's name do you expect of me? You got into a panic when you thought Fitz had put the finger on you and you ran, leaving me with the money, and setting things up to look as though I had killed you. You watched and would not lift a hand when Fred burned me and threatened to blind me. Do you want me to say I love you or respect you or have any feeling but one of horror and disgust? You're a criminal and a coward. But you're done now, Will; it's all over."

"My! My! Miss Holier-Than-Thou." Will refilled his sherry glass. "I know you through and through, Helen. I know what makes you tick. You're coming along with me tomorrow, first to the Hepburns and then to Las Vegas. When we've got rid of that hot money, we're going to my place in Mexico and you are going to be my loving wife."

He set down his wine glass and gathered up my hair in his hand, twisted it and wrapped it around my throat, as he had often done before. The golden fleece, he once called it, and now, with the old gesture, he drew me toward him and kissed me. I fought in a frenzy to free myself with the inevitable result that he simply tightened his hold, the braid of hair pressing harder around my throat. So I made myself relax. And at length he looked at me, saw the shuddering distaste in my face, and pushed me away from him.

"Self-righteous little fool!"

"Don't they ever haunt you, Will?"

"Who?"

"Ben and Harry Fitzhugh and the guard you killed?"

"That was not murder. It was self-protection. The guard pulled his gun first."

"But he didn't shoot. Did you see his wife on television? She said he had never hurt anyone. She asked—why?"

Will shrugged. "As for Ben, he was going to spill everything he knew. I could tell the signs. So I had to."

"You hung him, didn't you? Didn't it sicken you to see him strangle, or was his neck broken at once?"

"I—" Will's hand gripped mine. "How do you know that?" My mouth opened and closed. He twisted my arm behind my back and I gave a cry of pain. "How? Who told you about Ben?"

"That's not the question that should be bothering you, Will. To whom did Fitz report on you? That's what sent you scuttling for safety months ago, wasn't it? You were afraid of the murder rap."

"Okay. So I ran from a murder rap. Who wouldn't? But I wish to God I had made Fitz tell me who he'd confided in before I killed him. It's been sheer hell waiting for something to happen and yet my name never appeared in the news except for the stuff about my disappearance, and you and Fitz were supposed to be responsible for that. Nothing to connect me with the payroll jobs. Why didn't Fitz's company come out in the open?"

"I suppose they were afraid you'd just disappear and they wanted you, just as the police wanted you, for murder and theft; and the narcotics division for getting young boys hooked on dope."

Will reached for a handkerchief and I jerked away from him. He did not leave the couch, but the gun was in his hand. "Don't open that door, Helen."

I was beginning to realize that I had been mistaken in thinking that the Volkswagen and the Ford had been following me. If they had, someone surely would have come before now. I'd be silly to hope that Jill had understood what I tried to tell her. I didn't know whether to hope that Ronald would come or to fear that he would. He'd have no chance against Will's revolver. Or Marilyn might come. She had been watching me. She might have seen Will come home with me, and she at least had a gun.

"It wouldn't help you much to shoot me, would it?" I said.

"It wouldn't help you much either," he pointed out. "How about getting us something to eat? I've been going to those drive-in Taco Bells for days because no one notices you there. But I need some home-cooked food."

So I found myself putting thick pork chops in the oven to bake. Automatically I had prepared them as Will liked them, with slices of tomato and green pepper on top. Habits die hard. I wondered whether, for the rest of my life, I would go on planning meals to suit Will's tastes and looking for apartments that would please him. Then I recalled that in the morning the showdown would come when Mr. Hepburn's security officers appeared with the money. If Will managed to get away from them and I was still alive, I would probably spend the rest of my life in Will's hideaway in Mexico.

While I was busy in the kitchen, Will turned on my transistor radio. The gun lay within reach of his hand and he watched every move I made. An announcer was giving hockey scores and then he quoted some minor statement from a more minor statesman. A special committee had been appointed to make an indepth investigation into the increasing traffic in drugs. Local, state, and federal agencies were pooling their information and co-ordinating their efforts.

"Talk, talk, talk," Will said. "That's all it amounts to."

"Do you ever take drugs?"

He laughed. "I'm not such a fool."

"But where did you get it for Ben and Fred and the other boys whom you turned into addicts?"

"That would be telling. Anyhow, you're a big girl now and you ought to know that there's nothing a person can't get hold of if he is able to pay for it. Got any aspirin? My head is splitting."

I measured the distance to the door. "It's in the medicine cabinet in the bathroom. You get it. I can't leave the dinner right now."

"Uh-huh. You get it, Helen. I'm staying right here."

So I looked in the medicine cabinet and brought him the aspirin bottle and a glass of water. It was a natural, habitual gesture and he was aware of it as he shook out a couple of tablets and drank the water.

"Helen," he said, "oh, love, what a mess we've made of it!" There was remorse and regret for something that had been good and that had died between us. He stretched out his hand to me and I almost took it. But it was too late. I went back to the kitchen to lower the heat and cook some rice in bouillon as Will liked it. I was grateful for that moment in which I was able to grieve for the Will I had loved.

Then the moment passed and Will turned to another station on the radio, listened until he realized he was hearing a symphony and turned the dial again. As he moved on from station to station, I was vaguely aware of the confused fragments that represented the greatest and most expensive communications systems in the world.

". . . at a recent hearing the Senator . . ."

". . . with fifty passengers aboard. No word has been received . . ."

". . . a good chance at the pennant . . ."

". . . for a cleaner wash . . . for whiter teeth . . . for all-day protection . . ."

". . . the hearty meal your husband will love . . . the gift no girl can resist . . ."

"All right, dinner's ready," I said at length, and Will came to pull up a chair across from me. I set a plate of his favorite food before him.

He tasted it. "Who needs Julia Child?" It had invariably been his comment when I prepared one of his favorite dishes, but it didn't work now.

"One thing gets priority," he said. "We're going to have to find one of those dingy secondhand clothing stores in the morning. I need pants and shorts and shirts."

"I'll have to go to the bank to cash a traveler's check first," I said. "I don't have any money. Oh, perhaps a dollar in change." I hoped he would not insist on examining my handbag.

"I've still got most of the money you gave me. Aside from keeping Fred and his mother sweet and paying for my food and liquor, I haven't had much chance to spend it."

At first Will ate hungrily and then he began to push the food around with his fork. "I thought I was famished, but I don't seem to be able to swallow the stuff. It must be this damned cold."

"You had better take some more aspirin."

"You wouldn't be remembering that it makes me sleepy, would you?" He pushed back his chair and my heart leaped but he did not approach me. He went to lie on the couch while I cleared away the almost untouched meal and washed the dishes.

"Jinxed," Will said at last, when I had prolonged the dishwashing and clearing up as long as I could and had come back to sit in a chair that faced the couch. "Right from the beginning the whole operation was jinxed. Fred was in no shape to do the hijacking, so I had to handle it myself. Fitz had double-crossed me. Then he sold me out. The guard was armed. The money was marked. I had two dead men and Fitz said his company knew what I was planning and he had also kept someone else informed about the whole thing. So I had to run like hell. And the only discount man I knew of had died on me. It's taken all this time to find an honest man."

"What would you have done, Will, if I had been found and arrested for your murder?"

"Beautiful women don't have trouble with the law except now and then in the divorce courts. But I can tell you it was a hell of a shock when that snapshot of you appeared. A hell of a shock. Fitz had taken the picture. If I hadn't buried him myself, I'd have thought he was the one to give it to the press. So that's when I knew for sure that he had told the truth when he said someone knew about the whole set-up. You wouldn't think anyone could play such a dirty trick, would you?"

"You are really unbelievable, Will. You're so warped you can't even think straight."

He started and I started, too, and I realized then how edgy we both were, how little it would take for Will to lose control and shoot me.

"God damn it!" he shouted. "A flea! I had to walk away from a new Cadillac and discount eighty thousand dollars, and I don't dare eat in a good restaurant or sleep in a decent hotel for fear of being recognized, and I pick up a flea at the palace like some skid-row bum."

I remembered then how fanatically clean he had always been. He was disorderly and surrounded by clutter, but he was always freshly bathed and cleanly shaven and his linen was impeccable. Those months of hiding out in a filthy shack must have been a bitter experience.

"I saw John Crothers the other night," I said. "He was in a restaurant and when he recognized me, he headed for a telephone."

"Did he call the police?"

I nodded. "We—I did not wait to see whether they came."

"We? Who's the boy friend?"

"That's more or less what Crothers wanted to know. He took for granted it was Fitz, whom he'd seen at the apartment."

Will laughed. "I got a kick out of those stories about you and Fitz. The way our old neighbors built up that quarrel between us and talked about Fitz hanging around. And Crothers saying how beautiful you are, the kind men fall for. And he ought to know.

He'd been dizzy about you ever since he first met you."

"You needn't think I gave him any encouragement."

"Not the ice maiden. But I didn't interfere. The harder he fell, the more secure my job."

"You are really vile, Will."

"Come off it," he said irritably. "Whether you know it or not, you're a man trap. Remember Fitz? He was rocked off his feet when he met you. I never saw a guy fall harder. Sometimes I've wondered if the reason he tried to break me was in hope of getting you. Well, it's a cinch he'll never bother you again. As for Crothers, he reacted just as I had figured he would. He's the one who first reported your disappearance to the police. He didn't believe anyone would walk out without collecting such a big commission."

"I suppose you know you'll never again dare apply for a job selling cars."

"Hell! I'll never have to work again. We've got it made, love. I have nearly two hundred and fifty thousand smackers in Mexico City. With what I'll make out of the eighty thousand loot, we'll be set for life. Mexico's a cheap place to live." He yawned. "I've got to have some sound sleep so I'm going to lock you in the bedroom tonight." He laughed. "Don't look so damned frightened, as though you were an innocent schoolgirl, if there still is such a thing. Too bad I can't justify your coy fears, but that has to wait until I shake this cold. In the morning we'll get me some clothes and you'll arrange to pick up the money as soon as Hepburn removes it from the bank. And remember not to make as much as a single gesture because, believe me, love, where we go we go together. Then we'll drive to Las Vegas and see my man. Finding him was no picnic. They aren't listed in the yellow pages and they don't grow on trees. You don't dare ask about them because someone will figure you've got something to discount and move in on you. Well, we'll spend the night in Vegas at the motel where I made reservations several days ago and next morning a private plane will fly us to Mexico City. We won't be coming back here from the Hepburn house, so you had better do your packing tonight."

"I'm not going, Will. It is ridiculous for you to think for a moment that I would. You can take the damned money but you can't take me."

"You'll have to go."

"What good will it do you, Will?"

"Because, my sweet, you are going to have to disappear. The world is going to continue to think that you and Fitz have gone out into the blue. You'll never dare show your face in these United States."

"Haven't you forgotten something?"

"What's that?"

"Fred and his mother know you killed Fitz. They can blow your whole story apart."

Will grinned. "They won't be talking."

I stared at him. "What have you done with them, Will?"

"Made sure they won't cause me any trouble."

"You haven't killed them, have you?"

"If they are dead, they asked for it."

"But are they?"

"No, they are not dead," he said shortly and clearly. "Last time I saw them they were still alive."

"Where are they? I don't know what you intended to do with them, but you can't hurt anyone else. You simply can't!"

"Well, I'll be damned. They both knock you around and he burns you and threatens to blind you. The guy is a junkie and his mother has done more rotten things than you've ever heard of in your sheltered life. They aren't worth saving."

"But we have to! We have to! Where are they, Will?"

"Oh, shut up!" he snapped. "Get into your bedroom. I'm going to lock you in and then get some sleep. Get moving."

"Don't move!" The door had swung open and Ronald came in at a rush followed by Marilyn Wilson and

Keith Putnam, whom I had last seen when he took Ronald away from the barbecue, under arrest.

Will looked at them and then he jerked me around in front of him, with one hand while with the other he pressed his gun against me. "Stay where you are. One move and she gets it."

TWENTY

For a few seconds we were all frozen in position like figures in a frieze. Then there was a sharp report and Will's revolver fell out of his hand while blood spurted from his shattered wrist. He sat staring at it, slack-jawed.

Keith moved swiftly to pick up Will's revolver and Ronald lifted me away from him and set me down on a chair, my dress stained with Will's blood. He took up a position between us, though there was no harm Will could do me now. His face was empty with shock and defeat. His left hand clutched his right arm, trying to stop the bleeding, which was dripping on his dress and on the carpet.

"Nice shooting, Marilyn," Keith commented.

"You were a good teacher, Keith." She dropped her revolver into her handbag. "You okay, Helen?"

"Yes, I—thank you very much."

"That's my job. I work for the Treasury Department, Narcotics Division. Keith is in another branch, but our assignments converged on this case. I told Jack Mason all about it when he came to look at my license to carry a gun. I'm sorry we had to put you through all this. We nearly left it too late."

"How did you know about Will and me?"

"Once we had pooled what we knew, the whole story fitted clearly together. We figured that as soon as you got the money, Gates would either try to get you out of the country or—eliminate you. So we've had an eye on you all day. The roof of your car is marked with luminous paint so it would be easy to spot from the air. A helicopter had been watching you and pointing out the way. We had a pick-up truck, a Ford, and a Volkswagen keeping close to you until we discovered you were coming here. That made everything easier."

"Why?"

"For one thing," Keith put in, "this cottage is bugged. I did that the night Marilyn got you out of the place. And by the way, Mrs. Gates, we hadn't figured on getting you involved in that raid. Marilyn has been watching the hippie joint for weeks and the wires got crossed and the raid occurred a night sooner than we had figured."

"You bugged this cottage? Why?"

"I had you figured all wrong," Marilyn admitted. "I thought you and Ronald were working together and that you two had killed your husband. I thought you were both in the dope pushing racket because we had traced Gates and his dealing with kids. I had a line on him giving them dope and Keith was working on the payroll hold-ups and tracing stolen money. So we found we were working on the same problem and I figured that you and Ronald had taken over and eliminated Gates."

"But I never saw Ronald until just a few days ago."

"No one seeing you in his arms as I did would believe that," Marilyn said dryly, but she was amused.

Across the room Will took a long look at me, a longer look at Ronald, his eyes cold with anger. "You double-crossing little bitch," he said softly.

"Anyhow," Marilyn said, "we've been listening from my cottage. Jill came running to report what you had told her and we were expecting trouble."

"It's my fault we didn't break this up sooner," Keith said. "I had bugged your car, but I didn't know how much or how little Gates had talked. I wanted to hold off until we could listen to the tape."

"And I must say," Marilyn commented, "if Ronald

had spoken up sooner and told us who he was and what he was after, we'd have closed this case a lot sooner. But he was afraid Gates would get away if we moved too soon. Anyhow, I arranged with Jack Mason to set up the barbecue and ring Keith in so he could size you both up. He took one look at you and decided you were in the clear. Then he took Ronald in for questioning. Ronald told Keith the whole story, so we were ready to move."

"Then Jill did understand what I was trying to tell her. Did Jack—"

"Jack," Keith said, "wanted no part of this. He would have no hand in the bugging. We explained that we wanted to keep a very loose tail on you because we were after Gates. Jill raised hell. She said after the way you had saved her little boy twice, she wouldn't let anyone harm you."

Will still sat clutching his right arm, trying to check the bleeding. He looked at Ronald. "Aside from making love to my wife, what is your connection with this?"

"My name is Ronald Boyd Fitzhugh. You turned my kid brother Ben into an addict, you involved him in a crime, and you hanged him to prevent him from talking. My father died of a stroke when he learned of Ben's death. Because I had to go back to Europe on assignment, my brother Harry took over and tracked you down."

"Then it was true that Ben was Fitz's brother. He told me just before—" Will's face showed a growing horror, but whether for what he had done or what was to come, I could not guess.

"Harry wanted you dead to rights," Ronald went on. "He kept me informed by mail, day by day, until the day of the robbery. I was fairly sure you had killed him, because there was never another word from him. And then I—found his body. We've got a long score to settle, Gates. You wiped out my family."

"So that's why you made love to my wife, so she would lead you to me."

Ronald met Will's eyes steadily and for a moment no one moved or spoke. It was Ronald, breaking free from Will, who turned to Marilyn. "How did you get onto me?"

"You left your fingerprints on the spade when you —uncovered that grave. They are on file because of your war service."

"I thought it might be something like that."

"Then you knew all the time that it was Will," I said.

"All the time," Ronald admitted. "I did warn you that you would hate me for what I was doing. I had a lot of trouble persuading Keith and Marilyn to let me play it out my way and hold off until you got the money. I knew that would bring Gates out of his rat hole, and I wanted Gates."

"Looks like you've got him." Jack Mason came into the room. "I'm taking over now, Fitzhugh. You should have left it to me in the first place."

"This was my private feud," Ronald said.

"This is the law. I operate under the law. That's why I won't be a party to bugging. And there's no place for private vengeance."

"I didn't want vengeance. I wanted Gates out of circulation for life so he can't harm anyone else."

Jack stood looking down at Will in that bloodstained dress. "You are under arrest, Gates."

"What's the charge?" Will demanded. "You talk about law. Let's see a sample. You can't use anything you got by bugging the car or the cottage. You haven't a scrap of legal proof against me on anything. If you are making it a murder charge, where's your case? If it's the payroll thefts, who had the money? My wife. If it's distributing a little dope to kids, where's your evidence? You haven't got a thing you can use against me, and you know it."

"The electric cart you were driving this morning when you met Mrs. Gates has been picked up. There are dried bloodstains in it. The prints on the wheel are the same as the ones found at the shack. When we've got a sample of your blood, the stains will match. You were bitten when you tried to rob the Hepburn place, weren't you? We are taking you in for questioning about an attempted break and enter. That's for now. We're going on, Gates. Distributing dope. Payroll robberies."

"And murder," Keith put in. "If that revolver of yours isn't the one with which you shot the guard, I'll eat my hat."

For the first time Will looked startled.

"Believe me," Jack said, "we'll get it all. Now let's start moving."

I think perhaps the worst moment of Will's life was not the arrest, not even the awareness that there was nothing ahead of him but the gas chamber; it was having to stand up in that woman's dress, a grotesquely comic figure.

"Wait," I said. "Let me stop that bleeding." And though both Keith and Ronald protested, they did not interfere.

"Go ahead," Jack told me, but his revolver was in his hand in case Will should make an unexpected move. I prepared a tourniquet to stop the bleeding and cleaned out the wound the best I could. Only when I started to bandage Will's wrist and fragments of broken bone rubbed together did he scream like a woman.

"He's got to have a doctor," I said.

"All in good time," Keith remarked.

"But he's in pain. You can't—"

"Oh, yes, we can."

"Please, please," I appealed to Mason.

"Take it easy," he said. "They'll get a doctor for him as soon as he's been booked. They'll fix up his wrist. You can rely on that."

"Though small good it will do him," Keith commented.

"Okay," Mason said to Will, and again I stopped him.

"Wait. Will has done something to Fred Cook and

his mother. We've got to find out where they are."

Marilyn nodded. "We'll need them as witnesses."

"If they are still alive," I said. "Will has to tell you."

"If anything happens to them—" Mason began.

Will looked from face to face. Then he laughed. "They are your case, all the case you have, all the witnesses you have. You'll never find them." He began to cough. When he had finished, he fell back on the couch, panting, trying to get breath into his tortured lungs. I brought him a glass of water and held it to his lips until he could manage a few swallows.

"Thanks, love," he said, and he seemed amused when tears spilled down my cheeks.

"Where are they?" Mason asked as soon as Will had recovered.

He got up, swaying, his eyes glazed with fever. For a moment he seemed to be pitching forward from sheer weakness. Then he had Marilyn's handbag, had her revolver, and turned it on himself. As Jack Mason lunged for him, he pulled the trigger, knocking over the coffee table as he crashed onto the floor.

TWENTY-ONE

The trim young intern looked up. "He's got a scalp wound. That's why there is so much blood. He didn't hit a vital spot." He and his companion lifted Will's unconscious body onto the stretcher. "Looks like it would have been better for him if he had. Better guys than that die every day."

They carried him out on the stretcher and I could see them slide it into the ambulance at the curb.

"Stay here," Jack said. "I'll want to get your statements. I'm going up to the apartment to telephone."

Ronald and Keith and Marilyn and I waited in silence for him to return. There was no feeling left in me. I could see how incredibly tired Ronald looked, but there was a kind of relaxation about him, too, that I had not noticed before. He had carried to completion the job he had set for himself.

When Jack came back, he said, "We are all going to the station so you can make your statements." He turned to me. "Jill wants you to stay with her tonight after I bring you back. She's—it is the very least—and even today with a gun being held on you, you saved our kid again."

"Thank her for me, will you? I—I'll see later."

Ronald spoke to me for the first time. "Will you let me drive you to the station?"

"I—no—I—anyhow, can't this wait? What about Fred and his mother?"

"They'll put out a general alarm," Jack said.

"But that might take days."

"We haven't a clue," he reminded me. "You had better give me as complete a description of them as you can."

I did and he wrote it down. "Have you any suggestions, any ideas at all about where they might have gone or your husband might have taken them?"

"Not the slight— Wait, wait a minute! They are too disreputable in appearance to be received at any decent place and Will—it was the flea. Somewhere on skid row. He said a palace, jokingly, I suppose."

"No, you must be right. There's a dump called the Palace. Let's get moving."

This time Ronald did not suggest that I go with him, and I got into Marilyn's car while the three men went in the patrol car. As Jack drove off, I could hear him speaking into his two-way radio.

The Palace was a huge old firetrap on a street that advertised naked movies and so-called curio shops that must deal in almost every kind of contraband. A police car was at the door and Jack went over to speak to the men. He and the other officers were to go first; Ronald was to remain with Keith and do as he was told. I was to stay behind with Marilyn and not appear at all unless I was called on for an identification.

The men went into the building. The windows were filthy, the steps seemed never to have been scrubbed. Marilyn sat quietly behind the wheel of her car, but her eyes were alert. She spoke only once. "I'll be lucky if they don't break me for this."

"Why?"

"Letting Gates get hold of my gun. That is just about the worst thing I could have done. The department doesn't make allowances for carelessness like that."

"What will happen to Will?" I asked.

"How much do you care?" she countered. "If there had been a chance for him by killing you, he'd have done it tonight."

"Yes, I know. But I am his wife and I was in love with him and happy with him for three months. I can't just blot that out as though it had never been."

"You can damned well try," she said callously, and we did not speak again.

It must have been thirty minutes before I jumped nervously as I heard a siren and an ambulance drew up behind Marilyn's car. One of the policemen came out, spoke to the men, and then came over to peer into the Ford.

"One of you Mrs. Gates?"

"I am."

"You're to come along, please." He looked at Marilyn. "You had better come with her."

The lobby had a few worn chairs and overflowing ashtrays and it smelled of stale smoke and unwashed people. At a desk a short fat man with small eyes watched us as we went up the worn stairs. There was no elevator.

There was no one in sight on the second floor. On the third floor we saw a woman in an old coat worn over soiled pajamas coming out of a bathroom whose stench sickened me. On the top floor a door stood open. Ronald and Keith were in the hall and when they saw me, Ronald protested.

"I've already made an identification. It isn't necessary to put Mrs. Gates through this."

"It won't hurt her. This gal has guts as well as beauty."

At the sound of voices, Jack came out. He took my arm. "Okay. Now all you have to do is tell us whether you recognize this guy."

"Is he—?"

He led me into the room which held a narrow cot, with a pillow and a single blanket, a chair with broken springs, a small shabby bureau from which most of the paint had flecked. There was a bundle of clothes on the bed. I looked closer, bent over, because the face was turned away. His eyes were open, but he did not see me. He'd never see anything again. His mouth was open and a fly buzzed near it.

I nodded my head, swallowed, and wet my lips. "That's him. That's Fred Cook. Did he—?"

Jack steered me out, turned me over to Marilyn, and beckoned to the intern.

"Take him away," he said.

"Is he—did Will—?"

"He's dead, as you saw. Not very long, perhaps an hour, according to the intern. Overdose of some drug, probably heroin."

"And his mother?"

Jack opened the door of the next room. At first I did not recognize the woman who sprawled on the bed. Her hair was black as Marilyn's and her face was plastered with make-up. She was monumentally drunk.

"Well?" Jack asked.

"Yes. That's Fred's mother."

The woman looked up, squinting as she tried to see who we were. "Oh, Gawd, the cops! I ain't done a thing. Not a thing." Her eyes traveled on, saw me. "Mrs. Gates! I thought you was dead. I need a drink!" She reached for a bottle and knocked it on the floor. She scrambled around frantically for it and then realized that it was empty. There was another bottle on the table. She reached for it.

"I need a drink. We all need a drink."

Jack reached the bottle first, handling it carefully. He passed it over to one of the uniformed men who nodded and went out with it.

"You got no call to do that!" she snarled, her mood changing to one of belligerence. "You give that back! It's mine. Can't trust a cop. Stealing my whisky. If Will was here, he'd tell you it's mine. He gave it to me."

"We'll ask him about that," Jack said. "Come on." He helped her to her feet and Keith took her other arm as she stood swaying.

"I'm not going nowhere. I got to wait for Will. He's

going to bring Fred and the money. Our cut. He don't like it, but he's got to give us our rights."

"They couldn't come. We're going to find them."

"Oh, no!" she laughed and shook her head. "No, no, no. I'm going to wait here for Fred."

TWENTY-TWO

Something brushed lightly over my head and my hair and I turned my head away. It touched me again insistently, but as lightly as a butterfly. Then I heard Jill say, "Johnny, leave her alone! I told you to leave her alone."

I opened my eyes to see Johnny perched on the side of the bed, his blue eyes watching me anxiously, one small hand stroking my face.

"Hello, there," I said, and his face was transformed by his smile. He launched into a lengthy conversation of which I could not understand a single word.

"I'm sorry," Jill said. "I wanted you to sleep. He ought to be paddled."

"What time is it?"

"About noon."

"How on earth did I get here?"

"Jack and Ronald carried you in. And you didn't even stir when I undressed you."

"What a nuisance I've been!"

"Nuisance! When I think what you've been through—" She broke off, afraid of what she might say.

"What has happened? Do you know?"

"Well, I—Jack said when you woke up and after you had had something to eat he wanted you to make a statement. It won't take very long. Helen, when I realized you were afraid of that guy and trying to tell me, I was scared stiff. I locked Johnny in here in his playpen and high-tailed it to Marilyn's cottage because she had told Jack who she was when he checked on her license to carry a revolver. I figured a government agent could do something. And Ronald was there and that man Keith. So I hoped it would be all right. But then—gosh! It was awful when I heard those shots. I was terribly afraid for you. I never was so glad to see Jack in my whole life as when he turned up. I knew he could handle anything unless—it was too late."

After a leisurely bath and a change of clothes and a breakfast which I didn't want but couldn't refuse because Jill was so kind and had worked so hard to make it look attractive and appetizing, Marilyn came to take me to the police station. She wore a simple dark blue dress and her hair was braided and worn like a coronet on her head. She wore almost no make-up.

Like Jill, she did no talking about the things I wanted to know, but drove straight to the police station.

There seemed to be a lot of people, several men in uniform among whom I recognized Jack Mason, who looked like little Johnny when he smiled at me, and Ronald, who gave me one swift searching look and then turned away. There were two important-looking men in plainclothes, one of whom was introduced as an inspector and the other as a captain.

The whole thing was unexpectedly informal. "You understand, don't you, Mrs. Gates, that we cannot compel you to testify against your husband," the inspector said.

"Yes, I understand. But I realize—it can't go on. He must not be allowed to go on."

"Thank you."

With the inspector to guide me, I told them everything I knew from the day I had met Will. Now and then one or another of the men interrupted me to ask for more details or to clear up a point, but on the whole they listened quietly while a young policeman in the corner took down my statement.

"And then he grabbed the gun and shot himself." I leaned back on the hard chair, exhausted.

"That's all very clear," the inspector said.

"You have been an admirable witness," the captain told me. "Now there is one thing more. We would like to accompany you to the Hepburn house to get the money."

"Of course." I started to get up, sat down again. "Please. I have told you everything I can. I have done my best."

"We are sure of that. We know, too, what a strain you have been under, with your life threatened. Anything we can do—"

"Please tell me. How is Will?"

"That scalp wound wasn't deep. It will heal nicely. And though his wrist won't—that is, it could not regain its full flexibility even—"

"Even if he were to live." After a moment I said, "That's what you mean, isn't it?"

"Yes, that's what I mean," the inspector agreed. "You understand, don't you, Mrs. Gates, that your husband has committed at least four singularly cold-blooded murders and, if it had not been for you, undoubtedly there would have been a fifth victim."

"A fifth?"

"Ben Fitzhugh, Harry Fitzhugh, the guard, Fred Cook. And his mother escaped by minutes. That third bottle of whisky had been poisoned."

"Oh, God," I whispered. "Oh, God."

"Yes, quite. She's not a nice woman and she'll probably continue to cause us trouble and end by the state supporting her, but we couldn't let her die like that."

"Does she know about Fred?"

"We had her here an hour ago. She had sobered up but she was jittery. She was difficult at first until we told her about the whisky and then she opened up about Gate's activities. Couldn't talk fast enough. She seemed to be laboring under the curious delusion that by telling us about Gates she would be earning her cut of the stolen money. She has quite an obsession about her rights. And Fred's rights."

"Did she care terribly when you told her about her son?"

There was a curious silence and then the inspector said, "She says she is going to sue the town for her rights. She wants her cut and Fred's cut. She was quite noisy about it."

"If you are through with Mrs. Gates," Jack suggested, "I'll drive her back to my wife."

"We'll have to see Mr. Hepburn first. Are you ready, Mrs. Gates?"

"When you are."

There was a moment of orderly confusion while the police conferred and I found Ronald beside me. "You understand now why I used you to track down your husband. It wasn't just for Ben or Fitz or even my father who died of grief. It was for you, too, ever since Fitz met you and sent me a copy of the picture he had taken, and said you were the loveliest thing he had ever seen and you must not be allowed to stay married to Gates. Forgive me if you can. If not now, then perhaps someday—" He turned and went out of the station while I stared after him blankly.

II

There isn't a whole lot more to say. Later that afternoon an unmarked police car drove me to the Hepburn house and returned with the hatbox, its contents intact. I remained behind at Mrs. Hepburn's insistence.

It wasn't over for me, of course. I talked to the authorities until I was hoarse, filling in all that I knew, but Mr. Hepburn protected me from reporters and kept the newspapers away from me, and asked me not to listen to the radio or look at television. I was glad enough to agree. Without anything being said, it was gradually assumed that I would stay with the Hepburns. We were to go to New York for an indefinite time, but first there was the ordeal of the inquest into Fred Cook's death. There was much excitement apparently over the discovery and restoration of the stolen money not only from the hatbox but the money Will had put away in Mexico from previous hold-ups.

In all this time I had not seen Will. I knew he was in the hospital and that no attempt would be made to question him until his condition improved. He had double pneumonia and he was in an oxygen tent. Then one day there was an urgent telephone call. Will wanted to see me. The police said no. The Hepburns said no. I said yes.

There were reporters outside the hospital as Mrs. Hepburn's car drove up and men stuck cameras practically into my face as well as microphones. At my insistence I went in alone. The receptionist at the desk, the doctor, the nurses stared at me as I went toward Will's room.

"Is he dying?" I asked.

"Yes," the doctor told me. "He has a good healthy body and he could have lived if he had wanted to. I think he wants to die."

At the insistence of the police a man in uniform sat outside the open door. The nurse who had been bending over his bed, her finger on his pulse, looked around. There were tears in her eyes as she jotted the temperature on the chart and went out of the room.

"He is conscious," the doctor said, "but he is very weak." He pushed a chair close to the bed for me and backed against the wall, out of Will's sight, waiting.

Will's eyes were open. "Hello, love," he said, and this was the Will I had known, the gentle Will with the great laughing charm.

"Oh, Will!"

"Don't cry. I messed things up, didn't I? There was a kind of kick in planning these operations. I was riding high and I'd even got you. So what went wrong?"

He laughed so weakly that it was just the thread of a laugh. He answered his own question. "I guess everything went wrong." He looked at the oxygen tent over his bed. "It's funny how they are trying to keep me alive so they can put me to death. Damned funny. But I happen to prefer oxygen to gas, so I'm going out."

"Oh, Will!"

"Look, I have no right to ask, but it won't be long. Will you stay and see me out? Give me something beautiful to look at?"

His hand groped across the bed and I took it in mine. For a few minutes his eyes were on my face, though he was too exhausted to speak. Then they closed. When I started to withdraw my hand, his fingers tightened, so I sat still until they dropped away and the doctor came quickly to ring for the nurse and take my arm.

"Come, Mrs. Gates."

So I went out of the hospital, leaving Will alone.

III

The Hepburns took me to New York and set out on a determined program of theaters, music, ballet, and art museums. Once a reporter tracked me down at the Plaza, where we were staying, but Mr. Hepburn made short work of him. Several times people recognized me on the street and stared at me as they would at a movie actor or a politician or even a man on stilts, but it no longer mattered. I wasn't wanted for anything now.

On the whole I tried to put the whole tragic mess behind me, but I never succeeded. Once in a while I tried to understand how I had been so completely fooled by the stage-setting Will had prepared for his own presumed murder. I no longer loved him, but I didn't hate him either. I was just sorry.

Now and then I got gay letters from Jill Mason,

bearing imaginary but fervent messages from her small son and planning the things we would do when I returned.

Now and then I heard from Marilyn. In her last letter she said she had gone on seeing Keith and he was beginning to talk about winter weddings. Maybe she had better make hay before I returned to cut her out.

Everyone, it seemed, assumed that I would return, including the Hepburns, who wanted me to live with them until I married again, a possibility they mentioned frequently.

"I must say," Mr. Hepburn commented one day after having given me a disparaging look, "you had better marry in a hurry before you fade completely away. No one likes skinny women. You've lost how much?"

"Twenty pounds."

He muttered to himself and went out of the room. Later that night I could hear the Hepburns having a terrific argument and guessed that it was about me. The time had come for me to free them of all responsibility for me and pick up my own life.

When I made this point, neither of them, somewhat to my surprise, protested.

"Give it a week," Mr. Hepburn advised, "before you make any final decision."

It was only a couple of days later that Mrs. Hepburn suggested that, as we had separate plans for the day, we arrange to meet for dinner at 21 at eight. I had bought a new evening dress and, as though to cancel out a memory and make a defiant fresh start, it was of emerald green velvet.

"The Hepburn table," I said at 21. "They have a reservation." But there was only one person at the table and I stared at him in disbelief.

When I was seated Ronald said, "Shall we order? The Hepburns aren't coming, you know."

"When did you arrange this?" I asked.

"Hepburn called me and said you were losing weight and that I'd better not overdo it."

"Overdo what?"

"Trusting to time to help heal the wounds and give you back some faith in marriage as an institution. Anyhow, I couldn't have waited much longer."

All through dinner he talked determinedly about astronauts and foreign policy and baseball and his personal views on life in general. Once he broke off to say, "I'm just giving you an all-around view of the subject. I'm thirty-one and in excellent health. I earn approximately twenty-five thousand a year by writing on politics or whatever. It takes a lot of traveling, but it's interesting. Though if you prefer a stay-at-home existence, that could be arranged."

After dinner he got a taxi but, instead of stopping at the Plaza, he signaled one of the hansom cabs that wait to take romantic couples through Central Park. He put me in and covered my legs with a rather dubious blanket.

He hadn't even touched me. Now he turned to me and his voice was strained. "Have I been building too much, Helen?"

"Ron, have you forgotten that I am notorious? That picture marked, 'This Woman Wanted.'"

"I do. I really do."

"What's that?"

"Want this woman. Very, very much."

I thought of all those months when I had waited. "Well, I must say," I stormed, "it took you long enough to tell me so."

He laughed as he took me into his arms. Poor Will had been wrong about that, as he had been about everything else. I was no ice maiden.

HOW MANY OF THESE DELL BESTSELLERS HAVE YOU READ?

1.	**SLAUGHTERHOUSE-FIVE** by Kurt Vonnegut, Jr.	95c
2.	**RICH MAN, POOR MAN** by Irwin Shaw	$1.50
3.	**A WHITE HOUSE DIARY** by Lady Bird Johnson	$1.95
4.	**THE SENSUOUS WOMAN** by "J"	$1.25
5.	**SUCH GOOD FRIENDS** by Lois Gould	$1.25
6.	**SUMMER OF '42** by Herman Raucher	$1.25
7.	**THE DEVIL'S LIEUTENANT** by M. Fagyas	$1.25
8.	**THE HUMAN ZOO** by Desmond Morris	$1.25
9.	**VECTOR** by Henry Sutton	$1.25
10.	**DELIVERANCE** by James Dickey	$1.25
11.	**THE AMERICAN HERITAGE DICTIONARY**	75c
12.	**THE DOCTOR'S QUICK WEIGHT LOSS DIET** by Irwin Maxwell Stillman, M.D. and Samm Sinclair Baker	95c
13.	**HOW TO TALK WITH PRACTICALLY ANYBODY ABOUT PRACTICALLY ANYTHING** by Barbara Walters	$1.25
14.	**SURROGATE WIFE** by Valerie X. Scott as told to Herbert d'H. Lee	$1.25
15.	**THE BODY BROKERS** by Robert Eaton	$1.25

If you cannot obtain copies of these titles from your local bookseller, just send the price (plus 15c per copy for handling and postage) to Dell Books, Post Office Box 1000, Pinebrook, N. J. 07058. No postage or handling charge is required on any order of five or more books.

Foreboding mansions, moonlight and the moaning wind ... a setting for romance, intrigue and the supernatural

GOTHIC MYSTERIES

ALONG A DARK PATH	Velda Johnston	75c
BETRAYAL AT BLACKCREST	Beatrice Parker	75c
BLEAK NOVEMBER	Rohan O'Grady	95c
COME TO CASTLEMOOR	Beatrice Parker	75c
THE DANCER'S DAUGHTER	Josephine Edgar	60c
THE DEAD SEA CIPHER	Elizabeth Peters	75c
HEATHER	Maeva Park Dobner	75c
HUNTER IN THE SHADOWS	Jennie Melville	75c
I CAME TO A CASTLE	Velda Johnston	75c
IMAGE OF EVIL	Rosemary Crawford	75c
THE LIGHT IN THE SWAMP	Velda Johnston	75c
THE MAN IN THE GARDEN	Paule Mason	75c
THE MARK OF MERLIN	Anne McCaffrey	75c
THE MASTER OF BLUE MIRE	Virginia Coffman	75c
MEGAN	Mary Kay Simmons	75c
THE MUSIC ROOM	W. E. D. Ross	75c
THE PAVILION	Hilda Lawrence	75c
THE PHANTOM COTTAGE	Velda Johnston	75c
PRAY FOR A BRAVE HEART	Helen MacInnes	75c
THE PRISONER OF INGECLIFF	Jean Bellamy	75c
RING OF FEAR	Anne McCaffrey	75c
THE SANDALWOOD FAN	Katherine Wigmore Eyre	75c
SHADOWS WAITING	Anne Eliot	75c
THE SHUTTERED ROOM	Julia Withers	75c
SILENCE IS GOLDEN	Elsie Lee	75c
THE SMILING MEDUSA	Jean Muir	75c
THE WITCH OF BLACKBIRD POND	Elizabeth G. Speare	75c
THE YELLOW GOLD OF TIRYNS	Helena Osborne	75c

DELL BOOKS

If you cannot obtain copies of these titles from your local booksel send the price (plus 15c per copy for handling and postage) to D Post Office Box 1000, Pinebrook, N. J. 07058. No postage or handl is required on any order of five or more books.